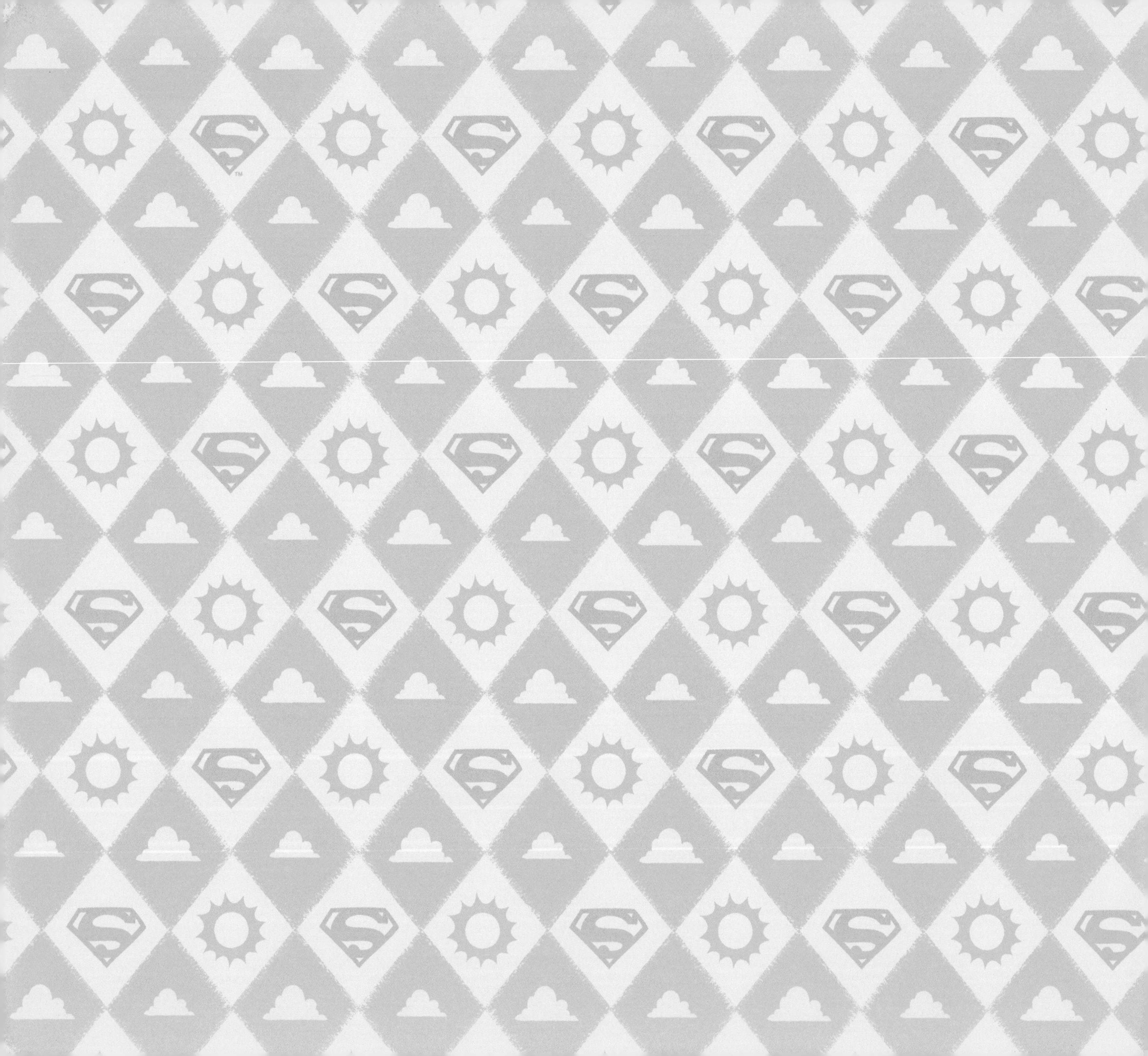

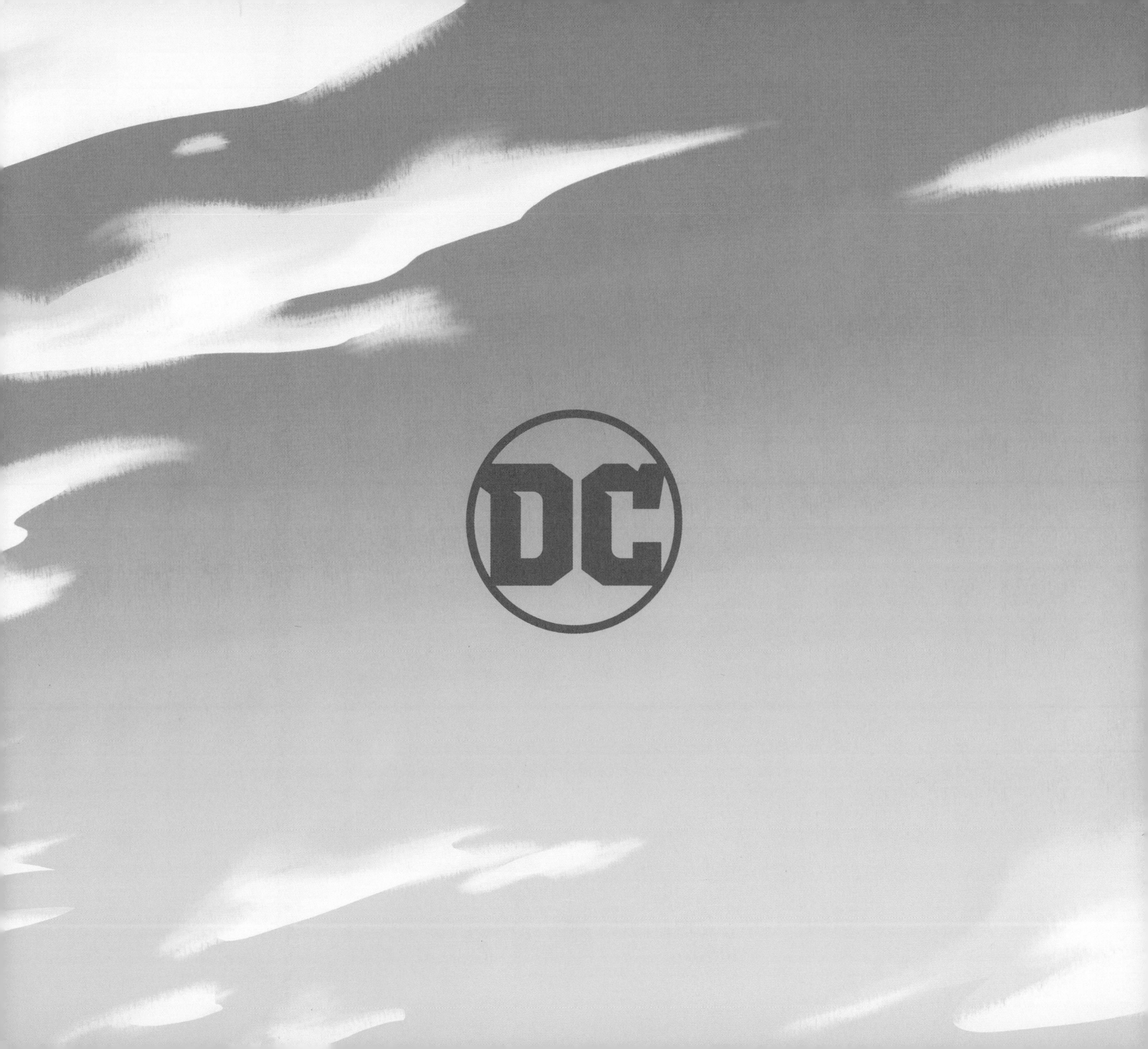

Good Morning, Superman is published by
Picture Window Books
a Capstone imprint
1710 Roe Crest Drive
North Mankato, Minnesota 56003
www.mycapstone.com

STAR37926

Cataloging-in-Publication Data is available on the
Library of Congress website.

ISBN: 978-1-5158-0970-8 (hardcover)
ISBN: 978-1-62370-851-1 (eBook pdf)

Book design by Bob Lentz

Printed in the United States of America.
022018   000011

words by **MICHAEL DAHL**

pictures by **OMAR LOZANO**

GOOD MORNING, SUPERMAN ™

Superman created by
JERRY SIEGEL and **JOE SHUSTER**
by special arrangement with the Jerry Siegel family

PICTURE WINDOW BOOKS
a Capstone imprint

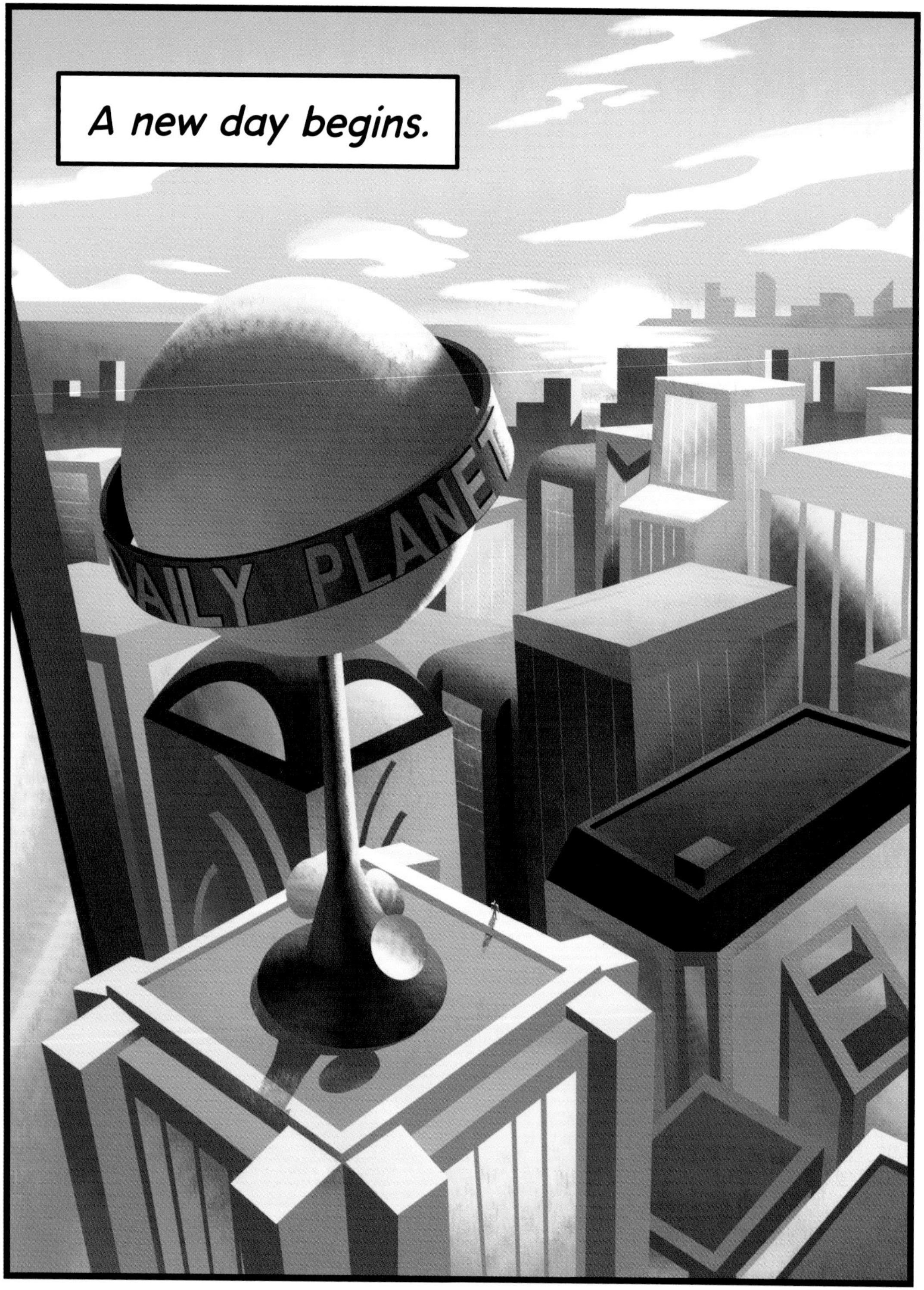
A new day begins.
AILY PLANE

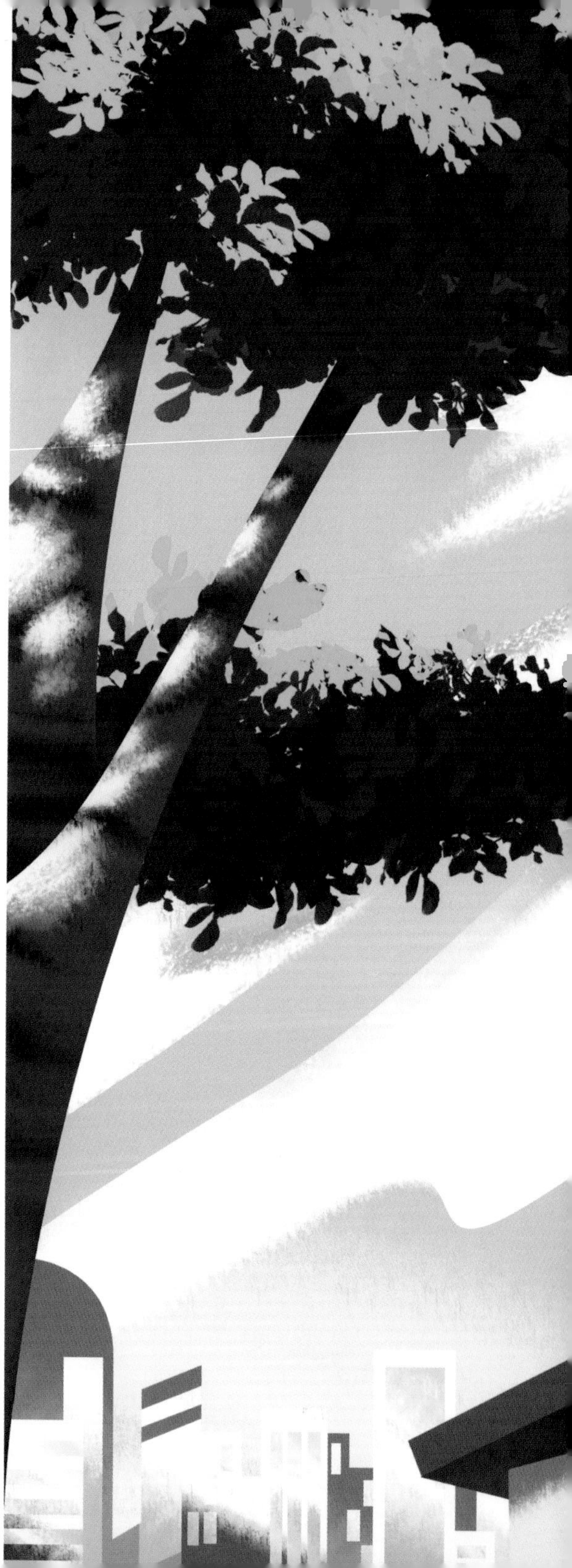

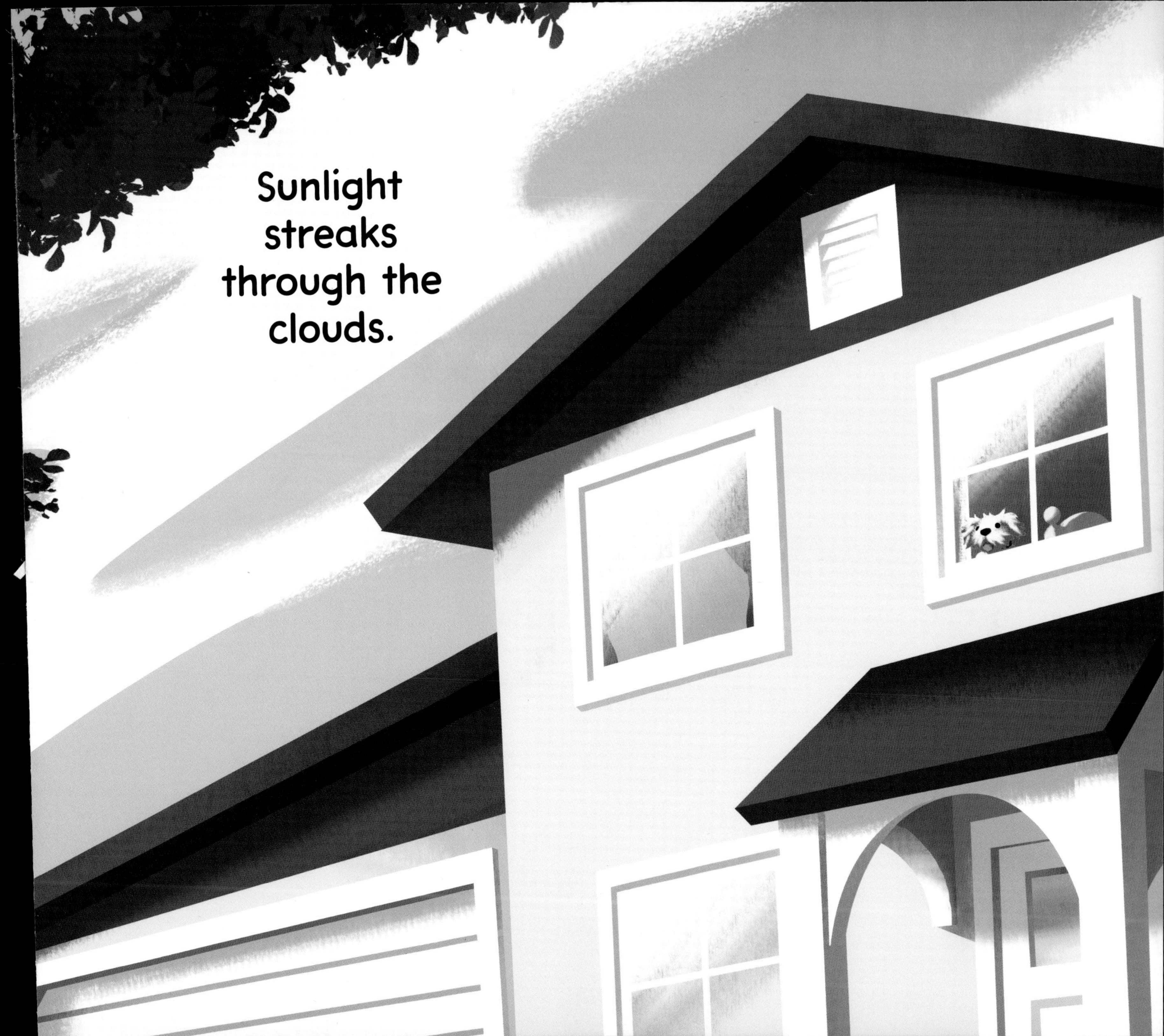

Sunlight streaks through the clouds.

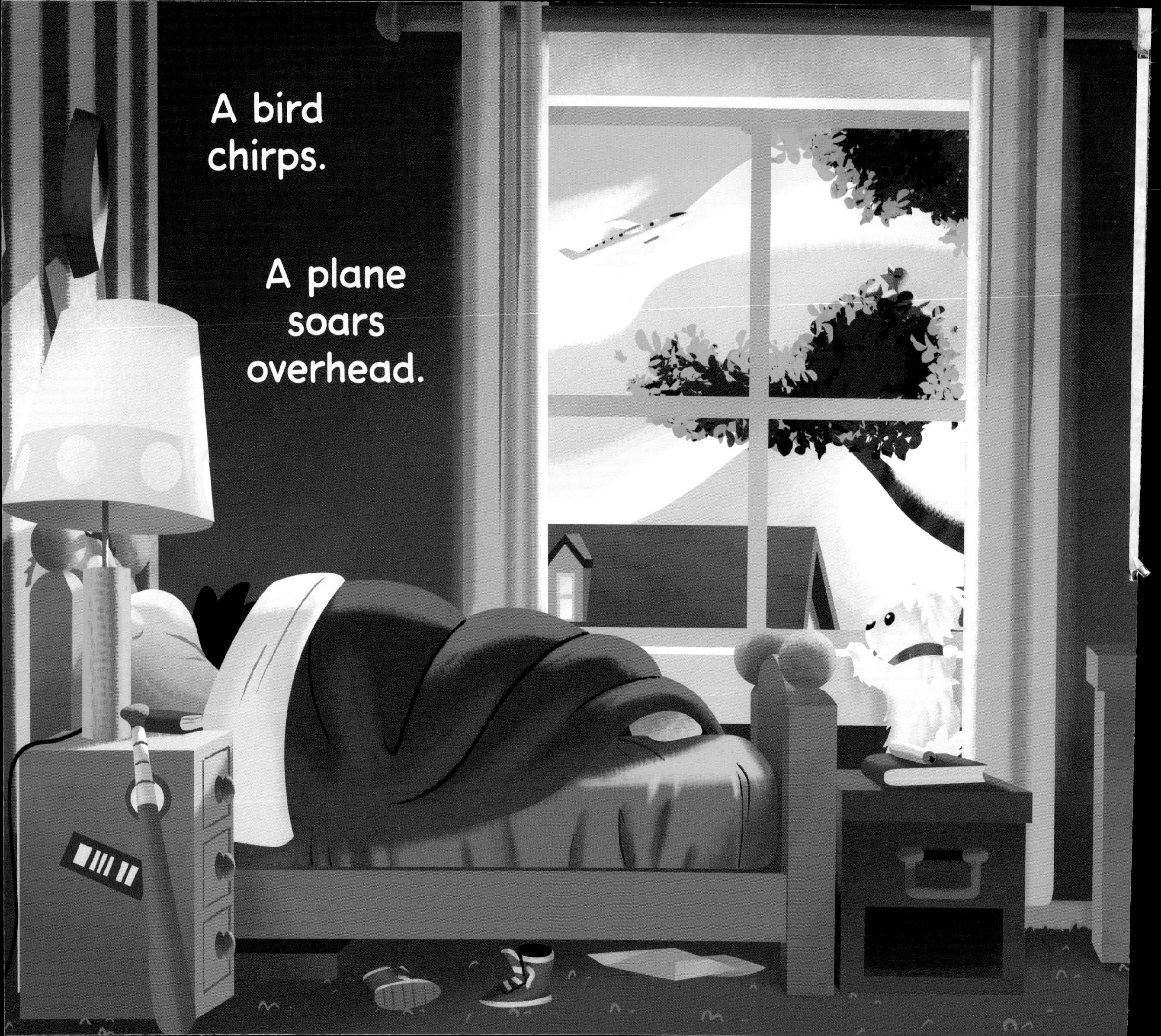

A bird
chirps.

A plane
soars
overhead.

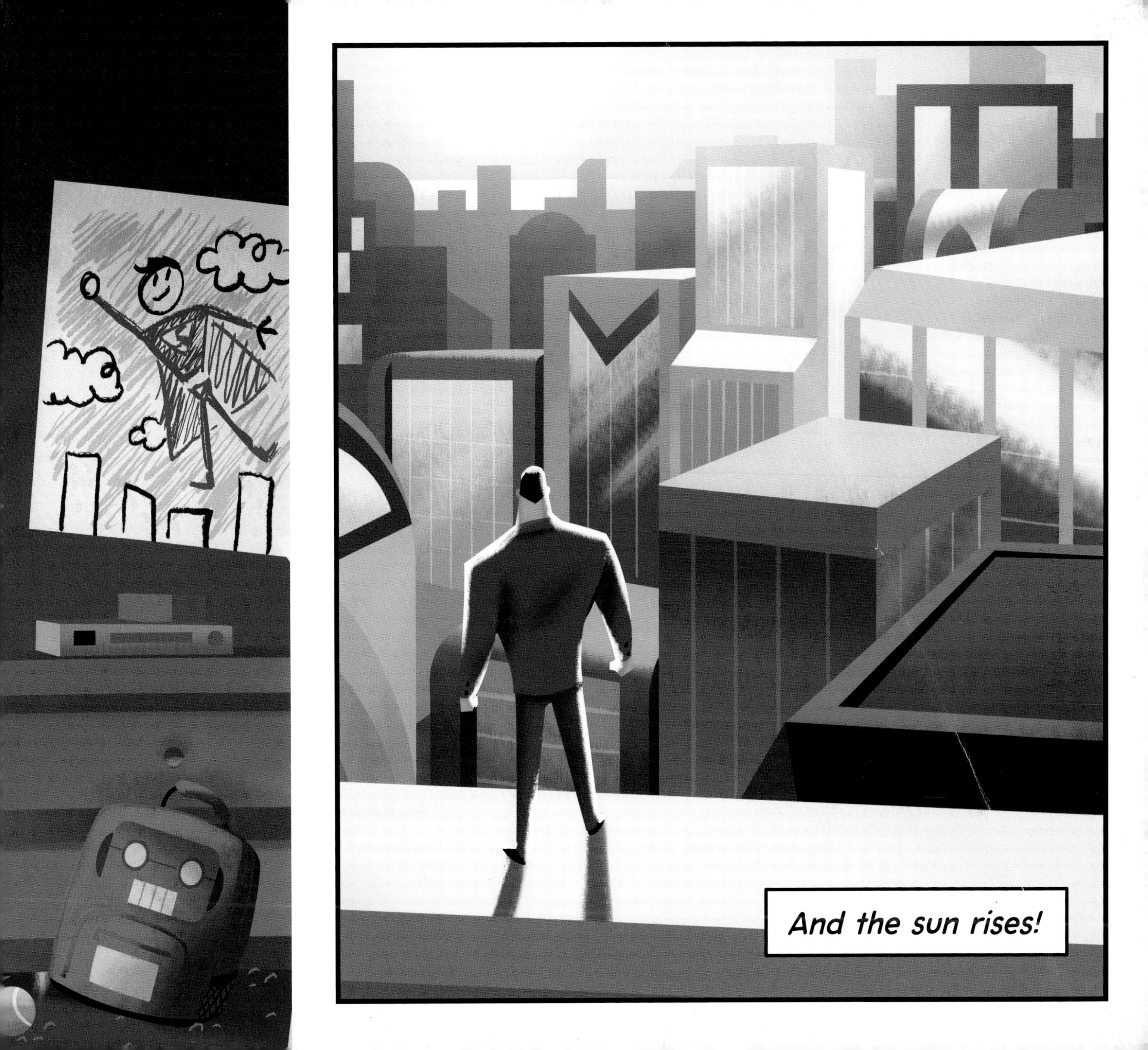
And the sun rises!

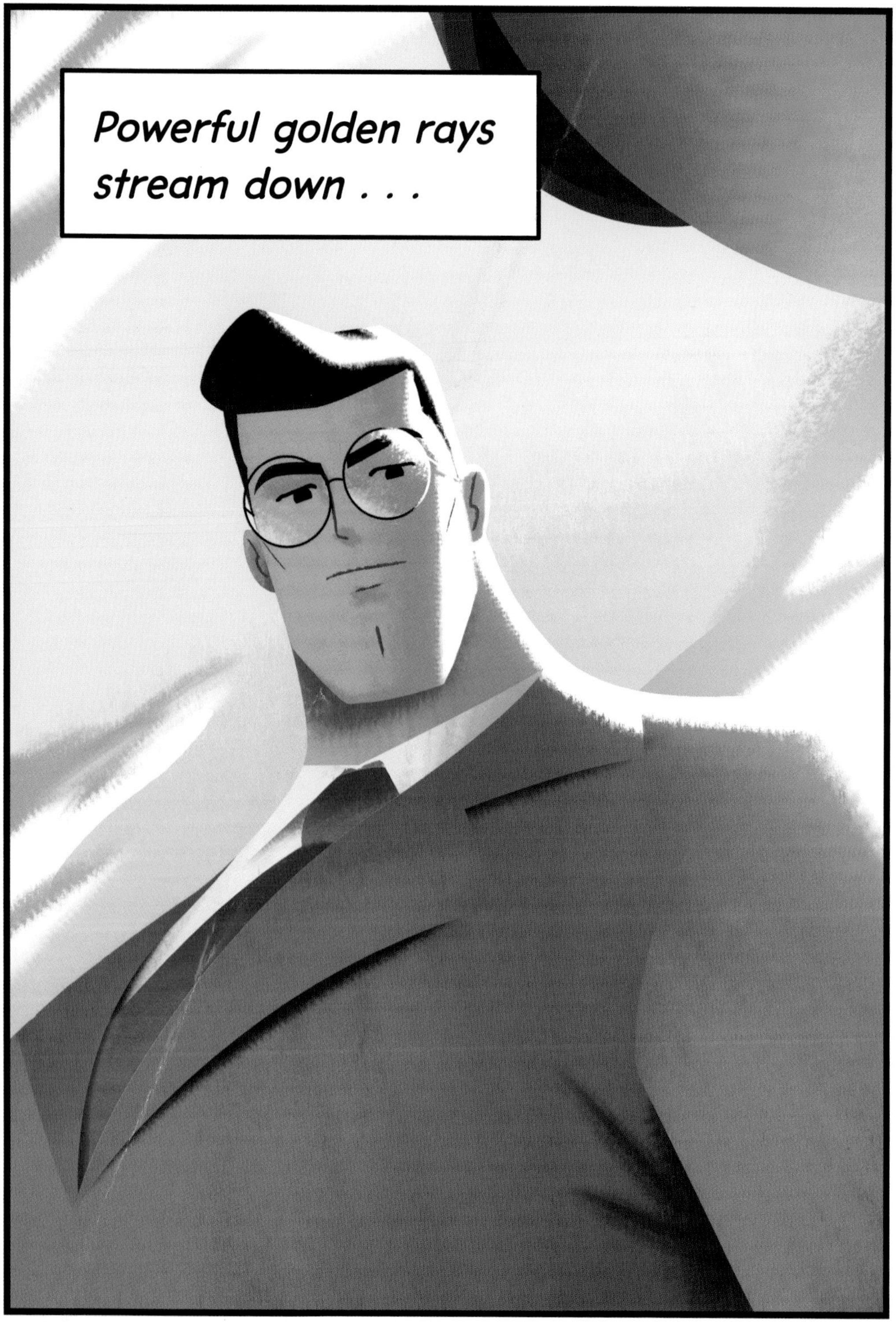
Powerful golden rays stream down . . .

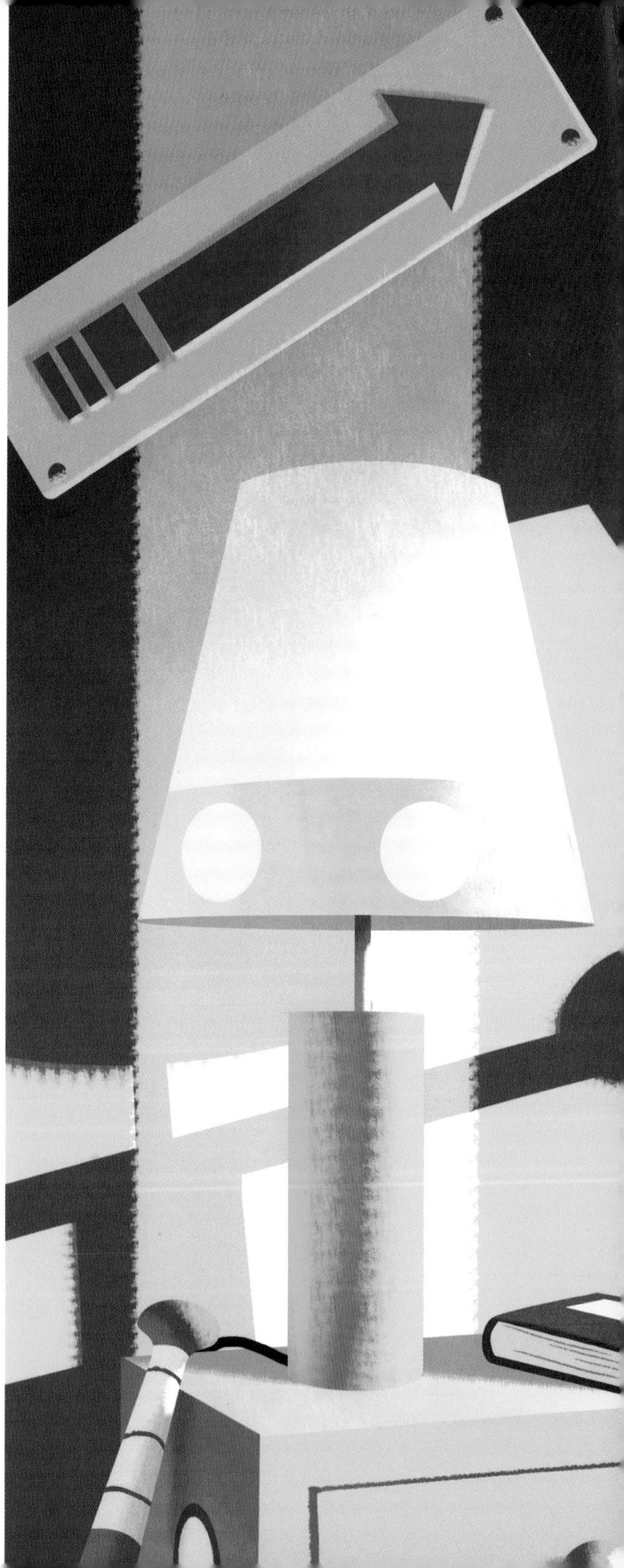

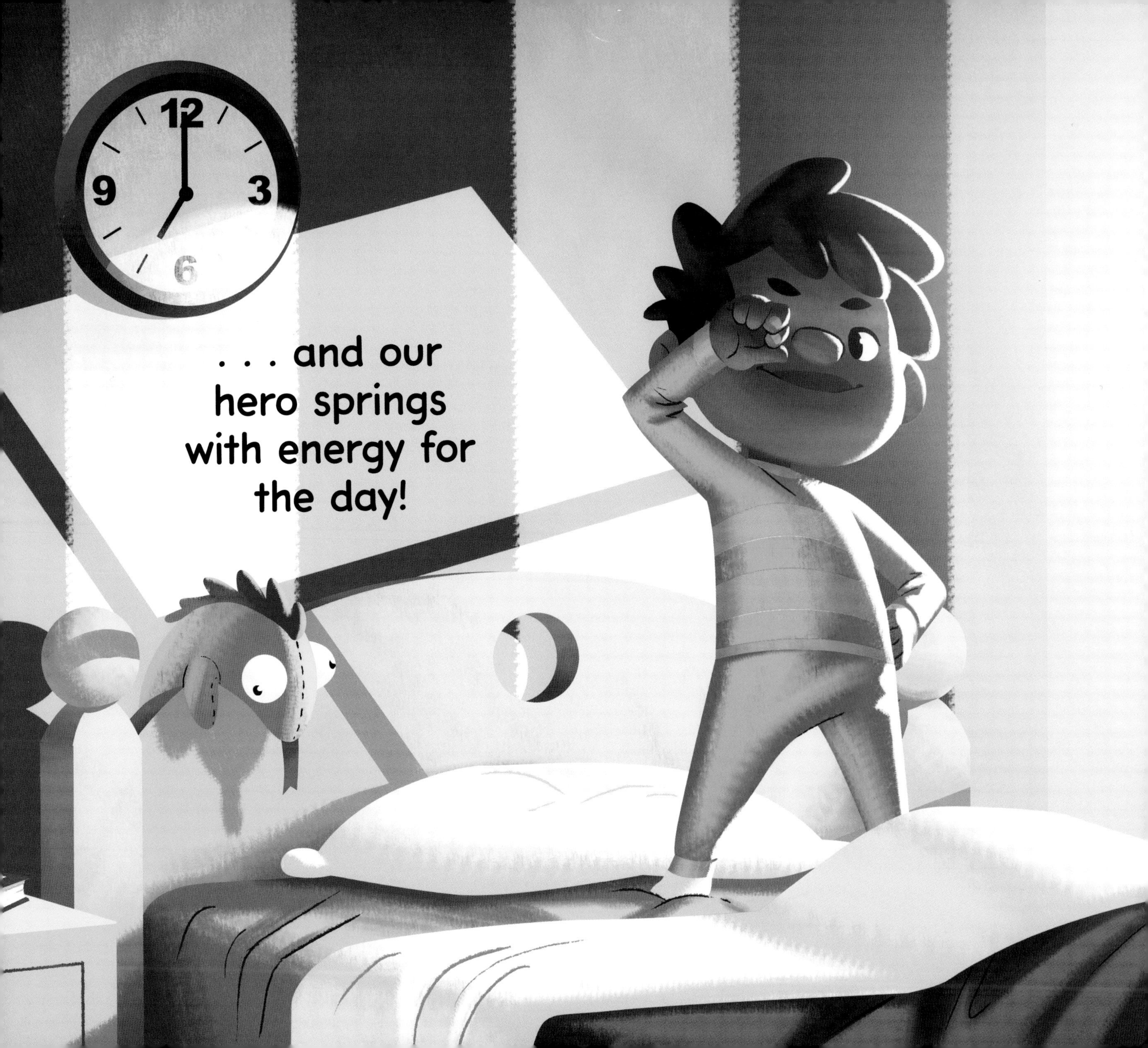
12
9
3
6

. . . and our
hero springs
with energy for
the day!

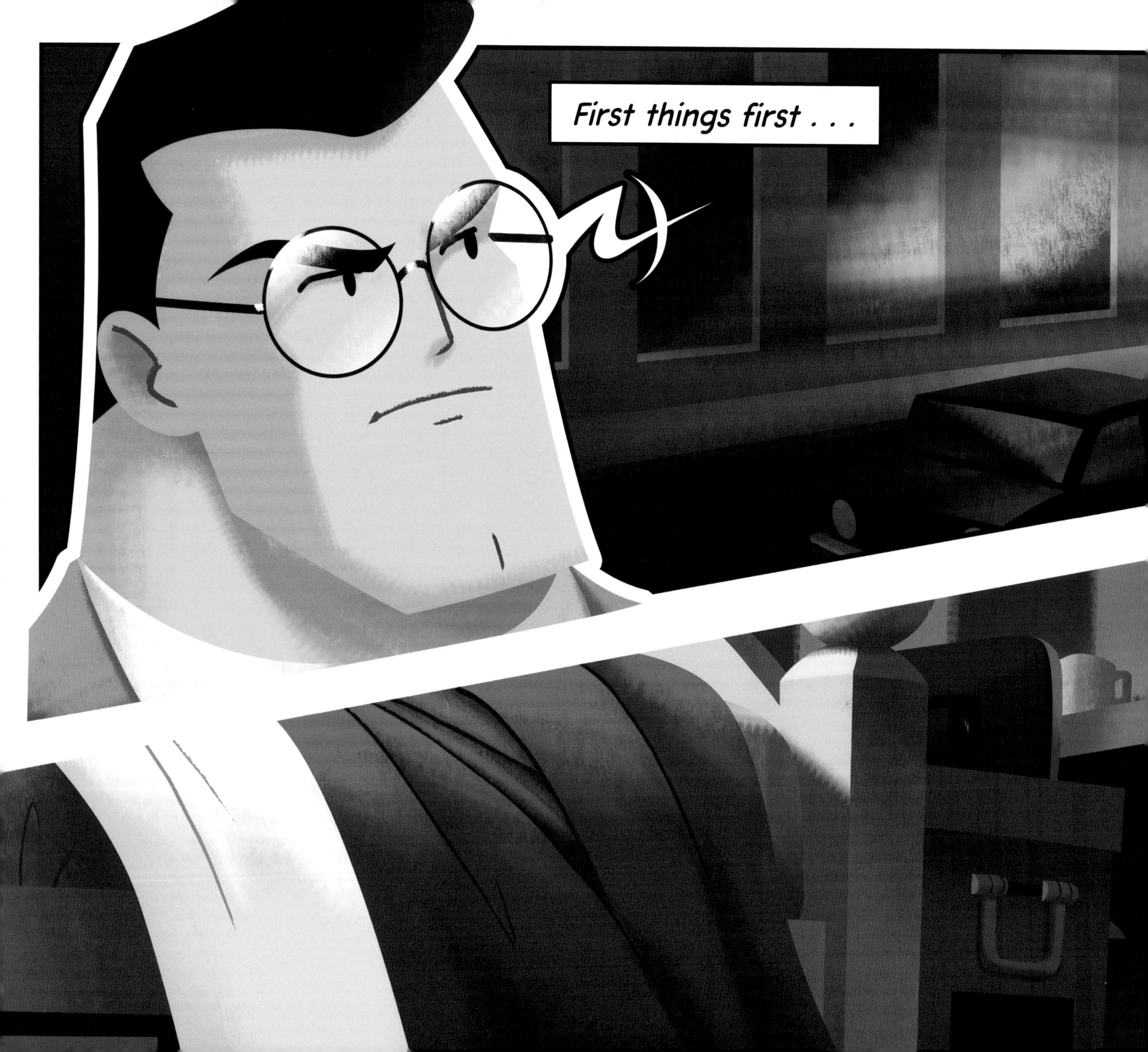
First things first . . .

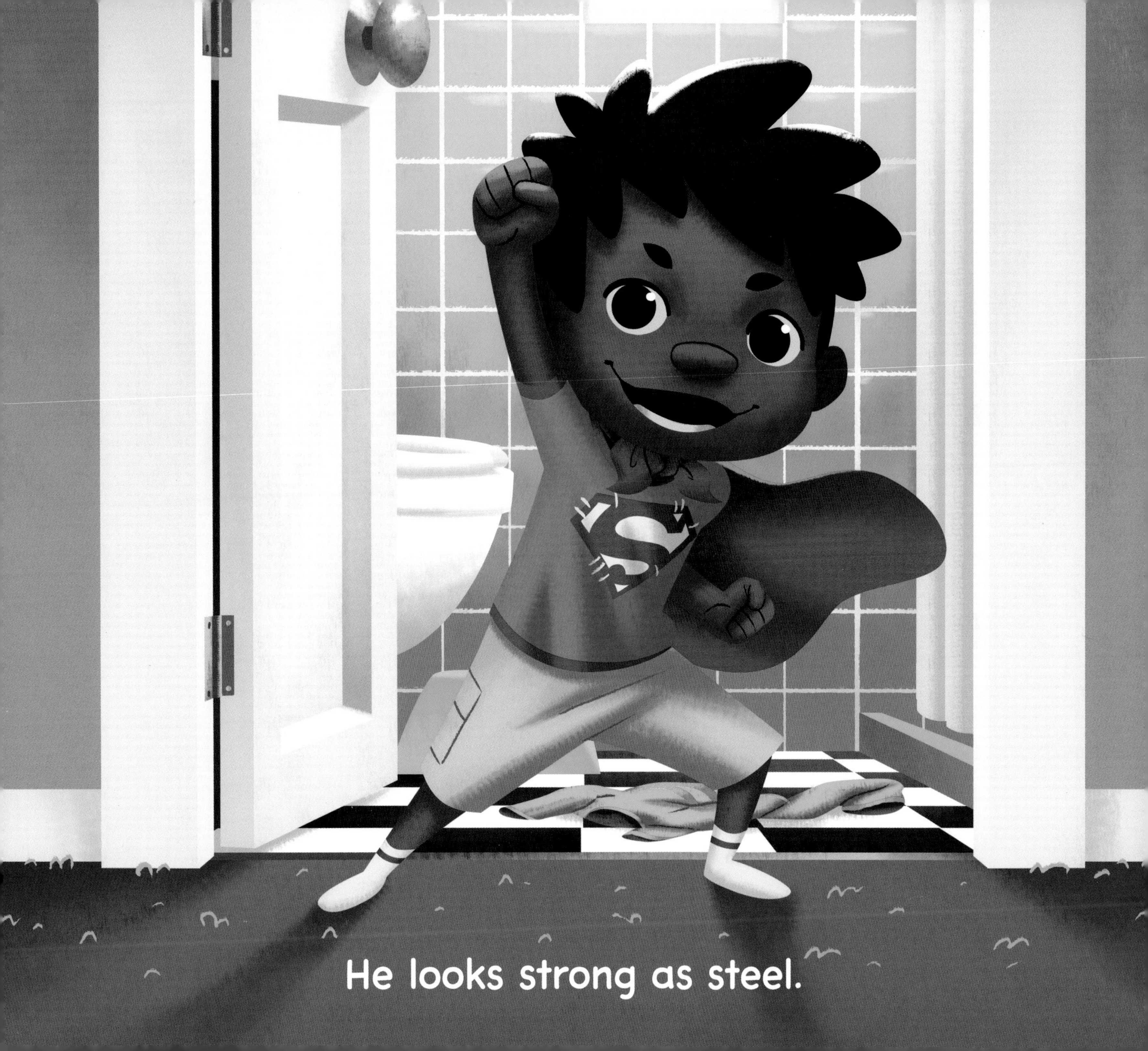

He looks strong as steel.

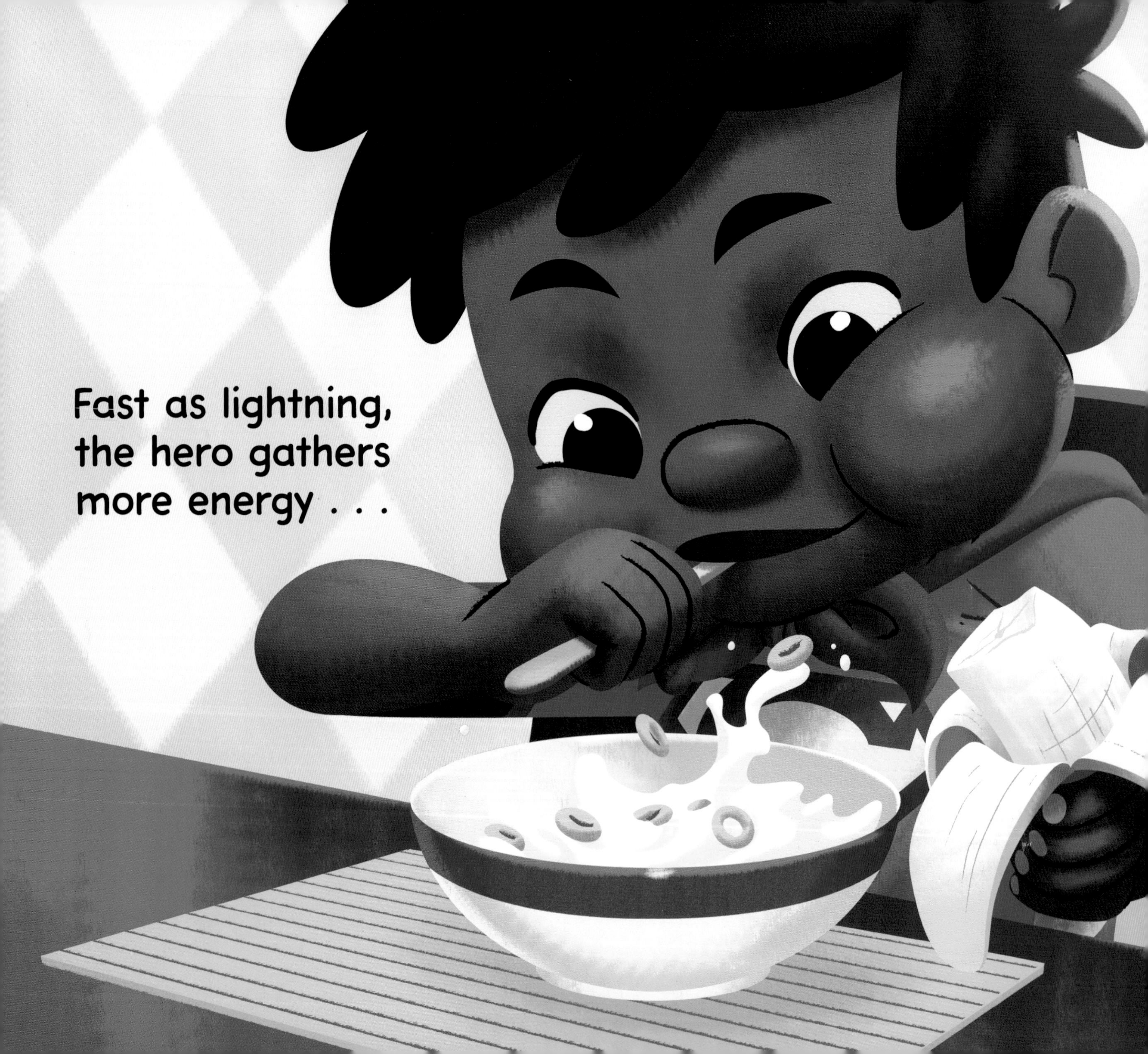

Fast as lightning,
the hero gathers
more energy . . .

WHOOSH!!

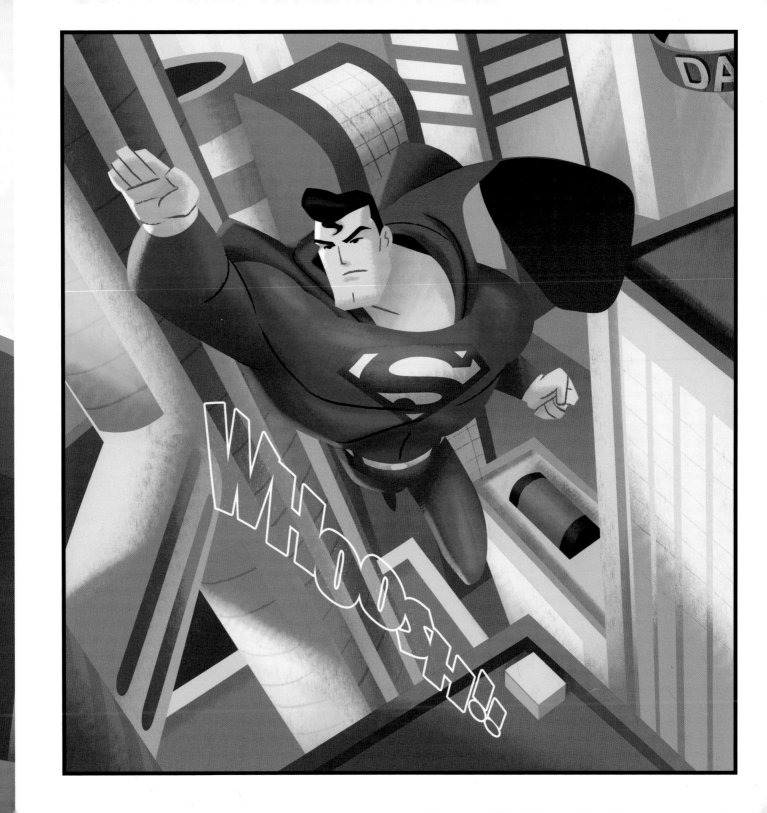

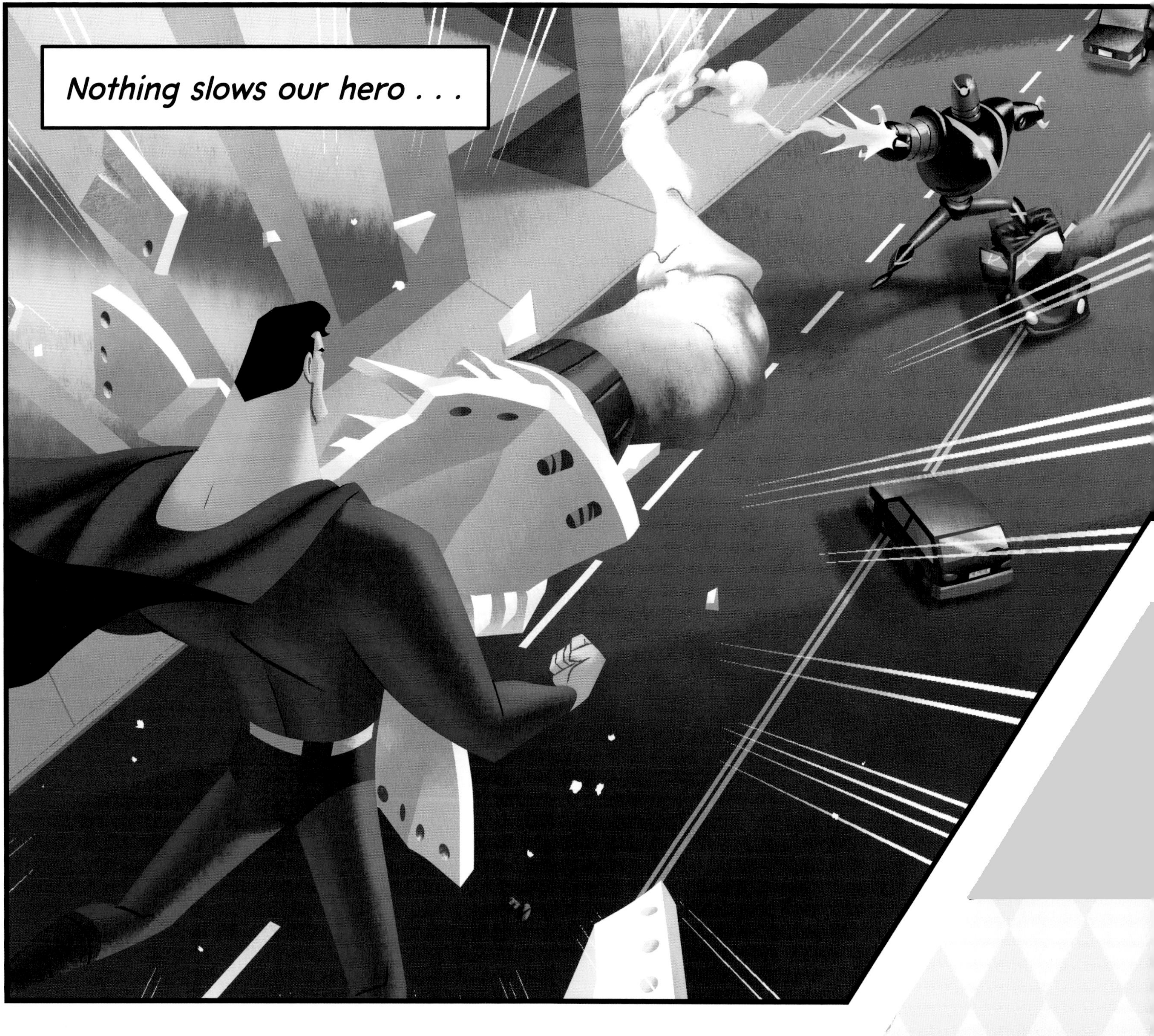
Nothing slows our hero . . .

. . . when he's on a mission!

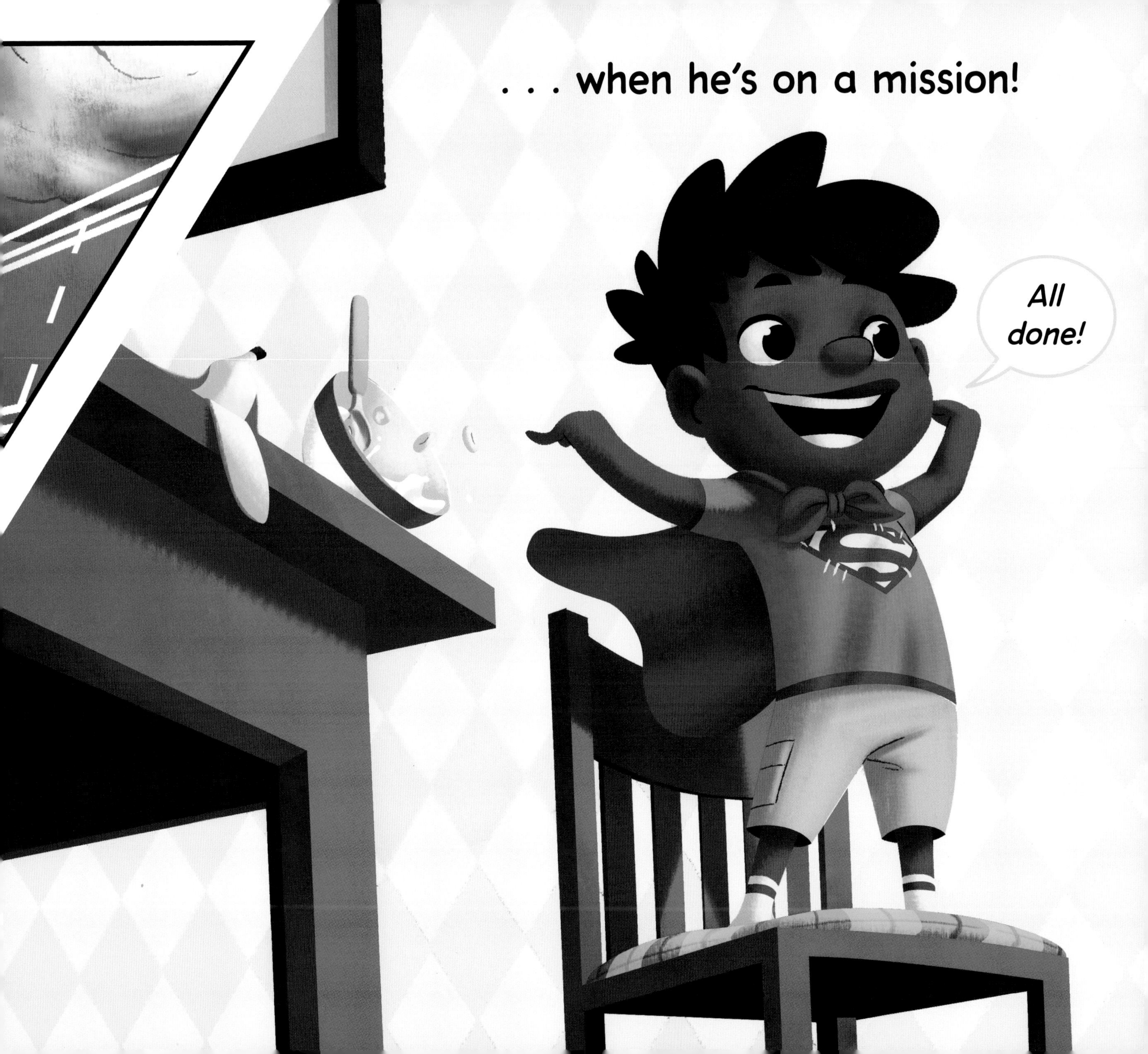
All done!

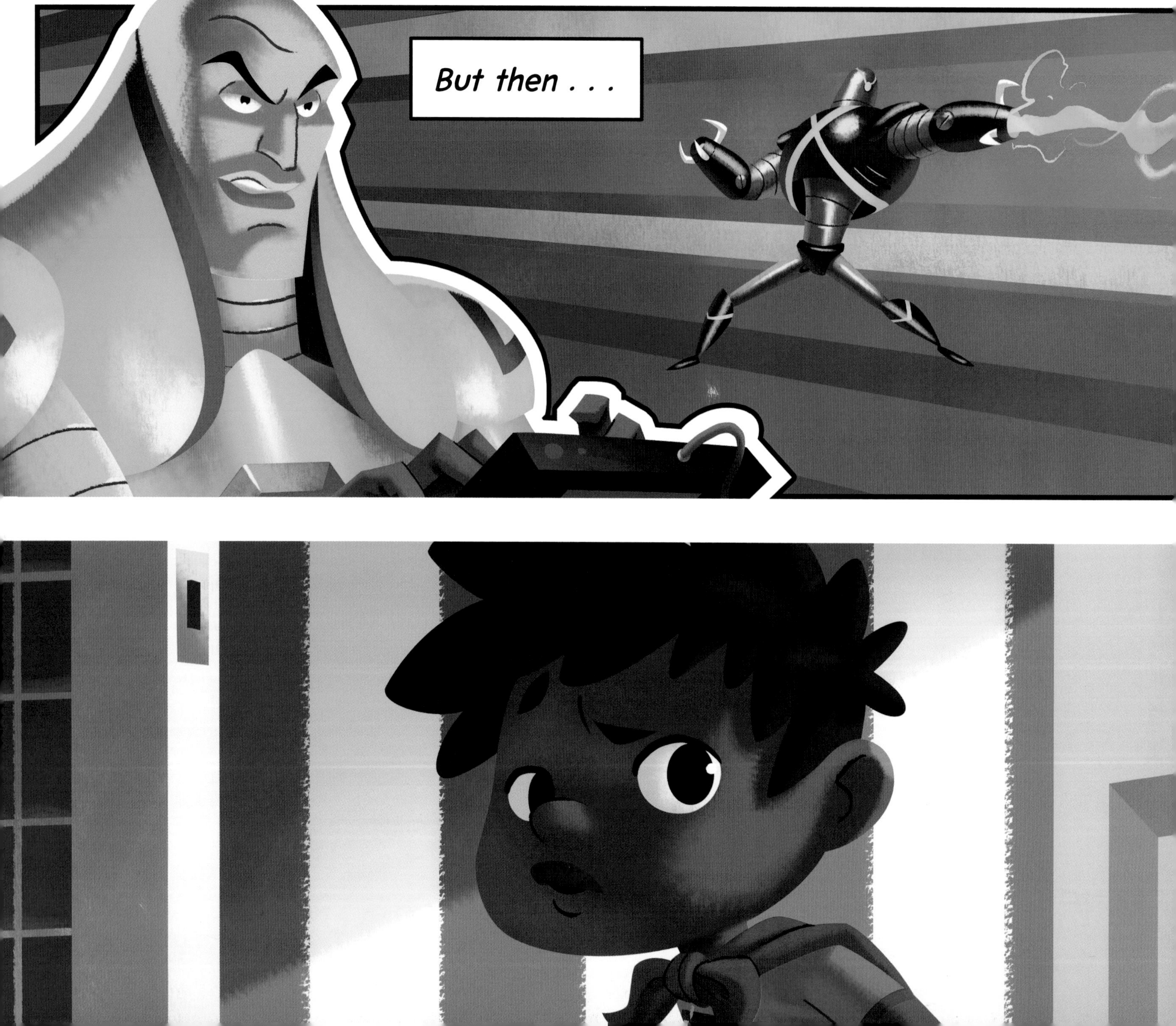
But then . . .

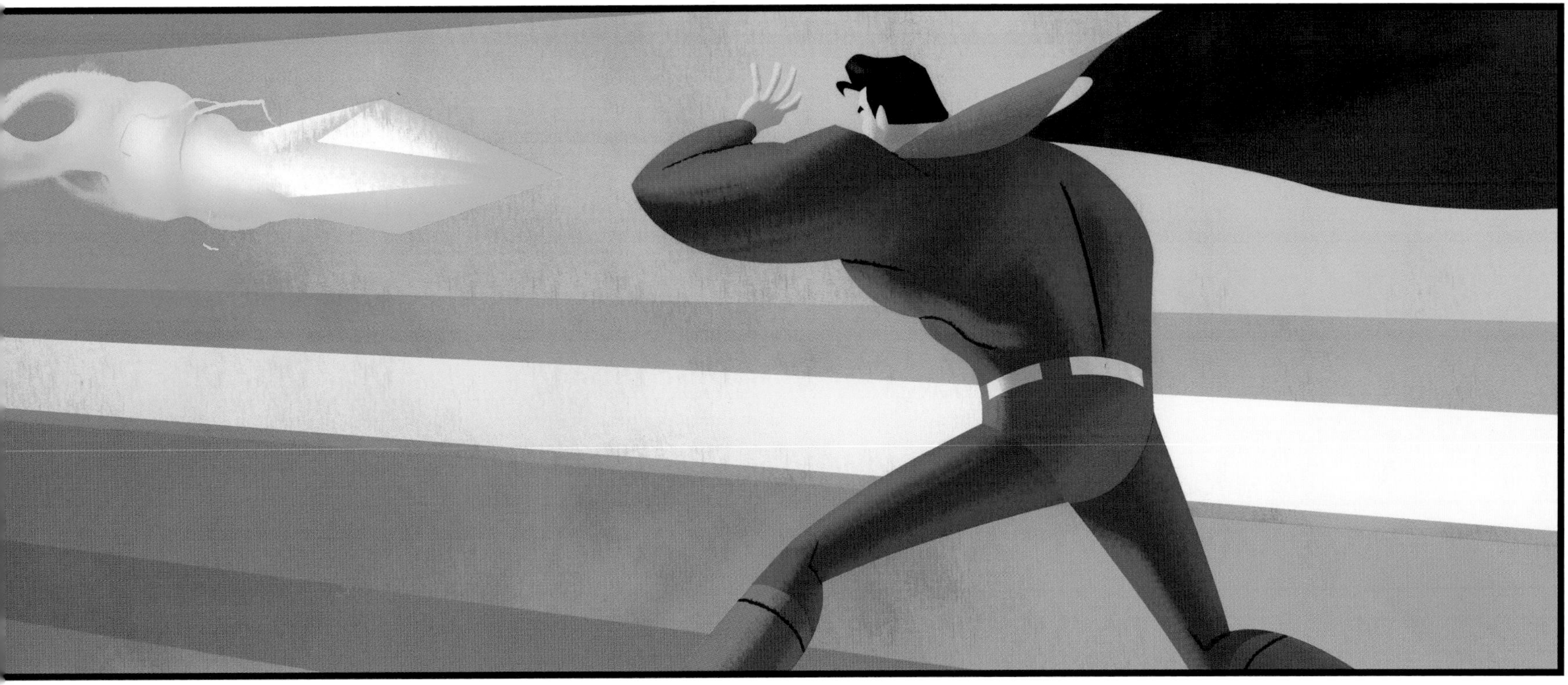

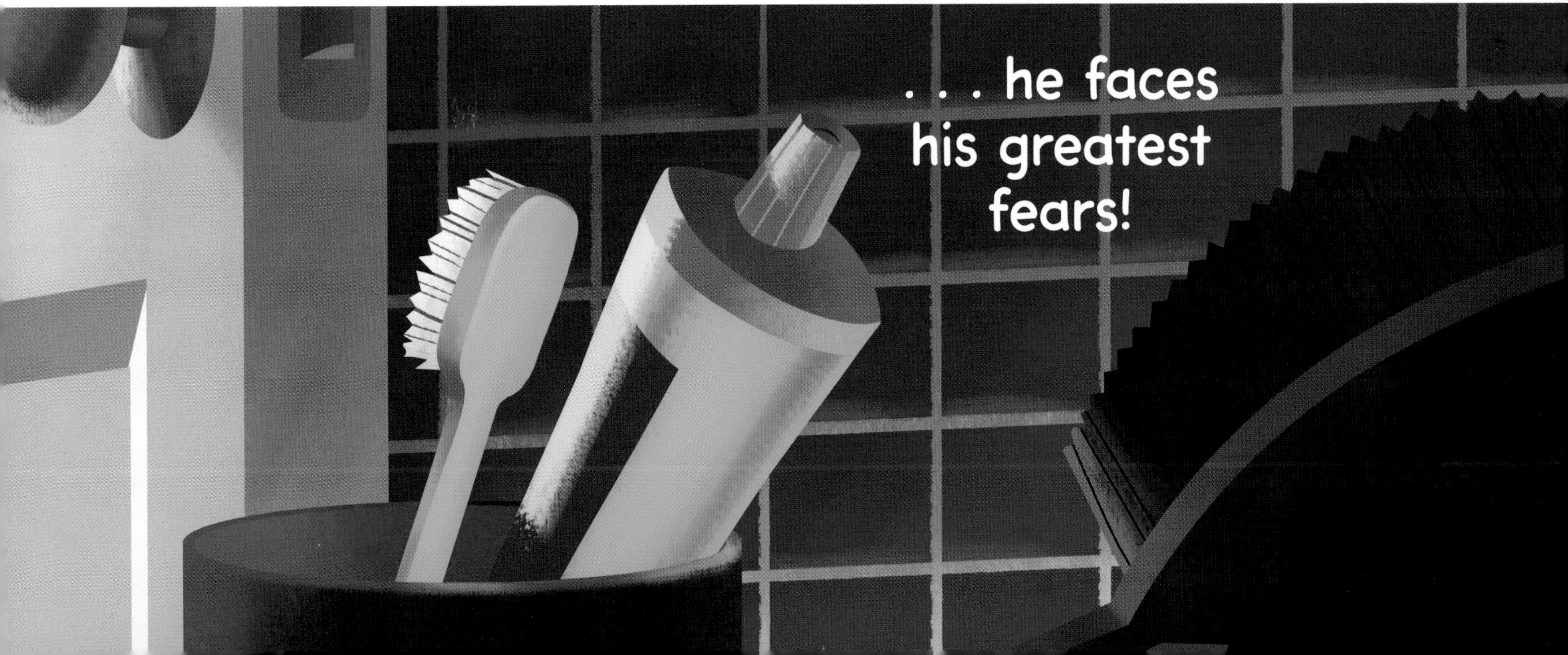
. . . he faces
his greatest
fears!

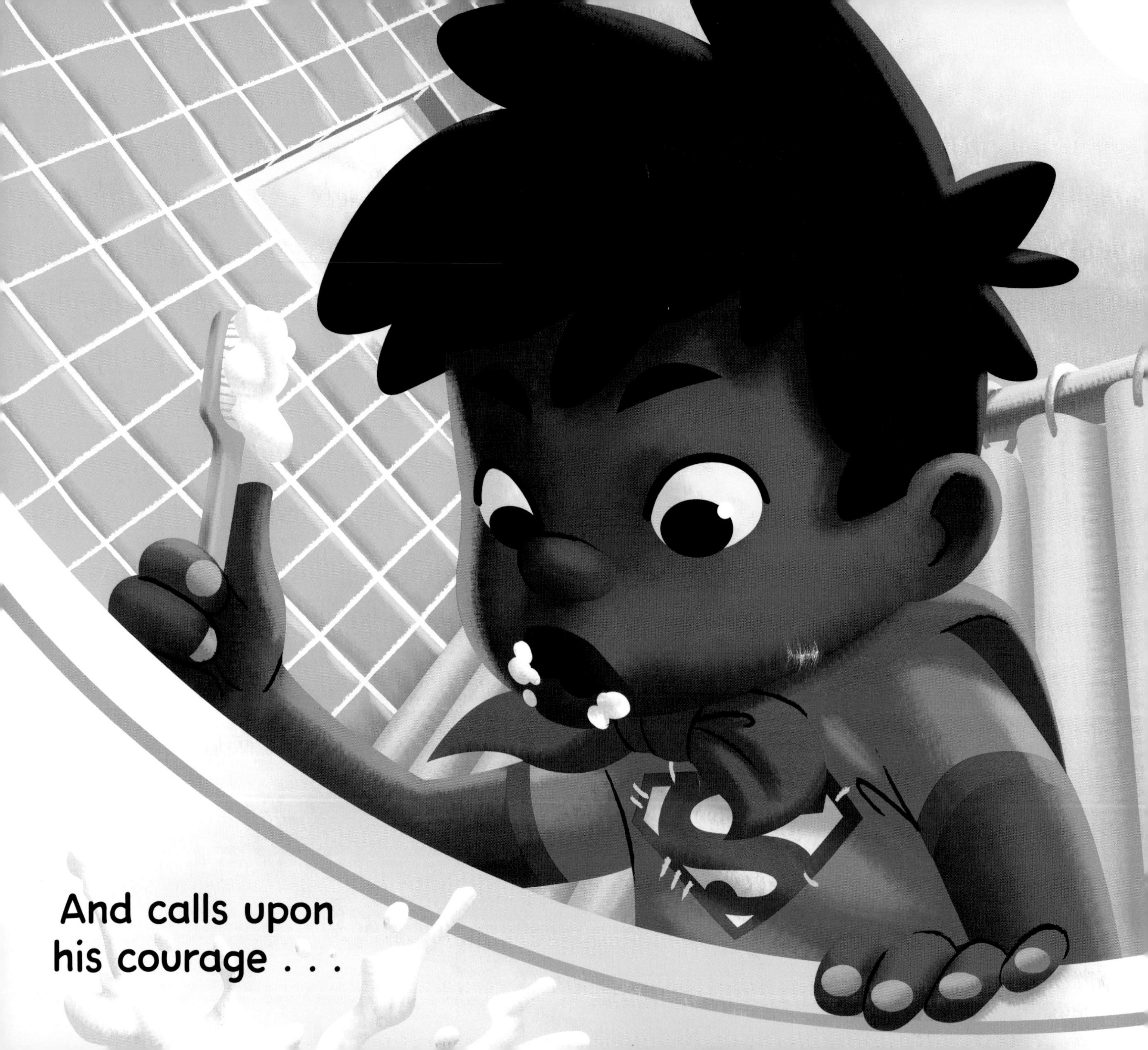

And calls upon
his courage . . .

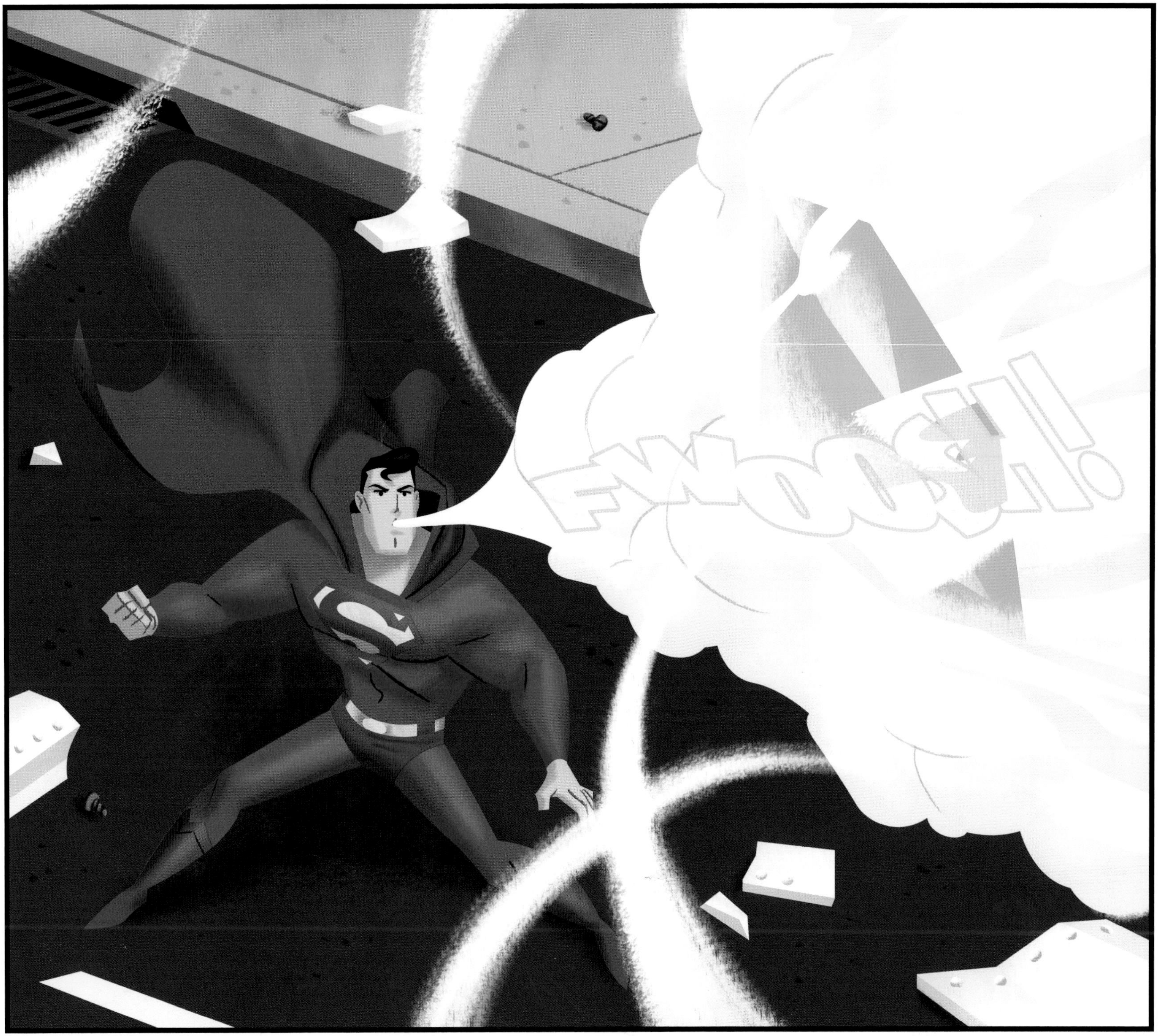
FWOOSH!!

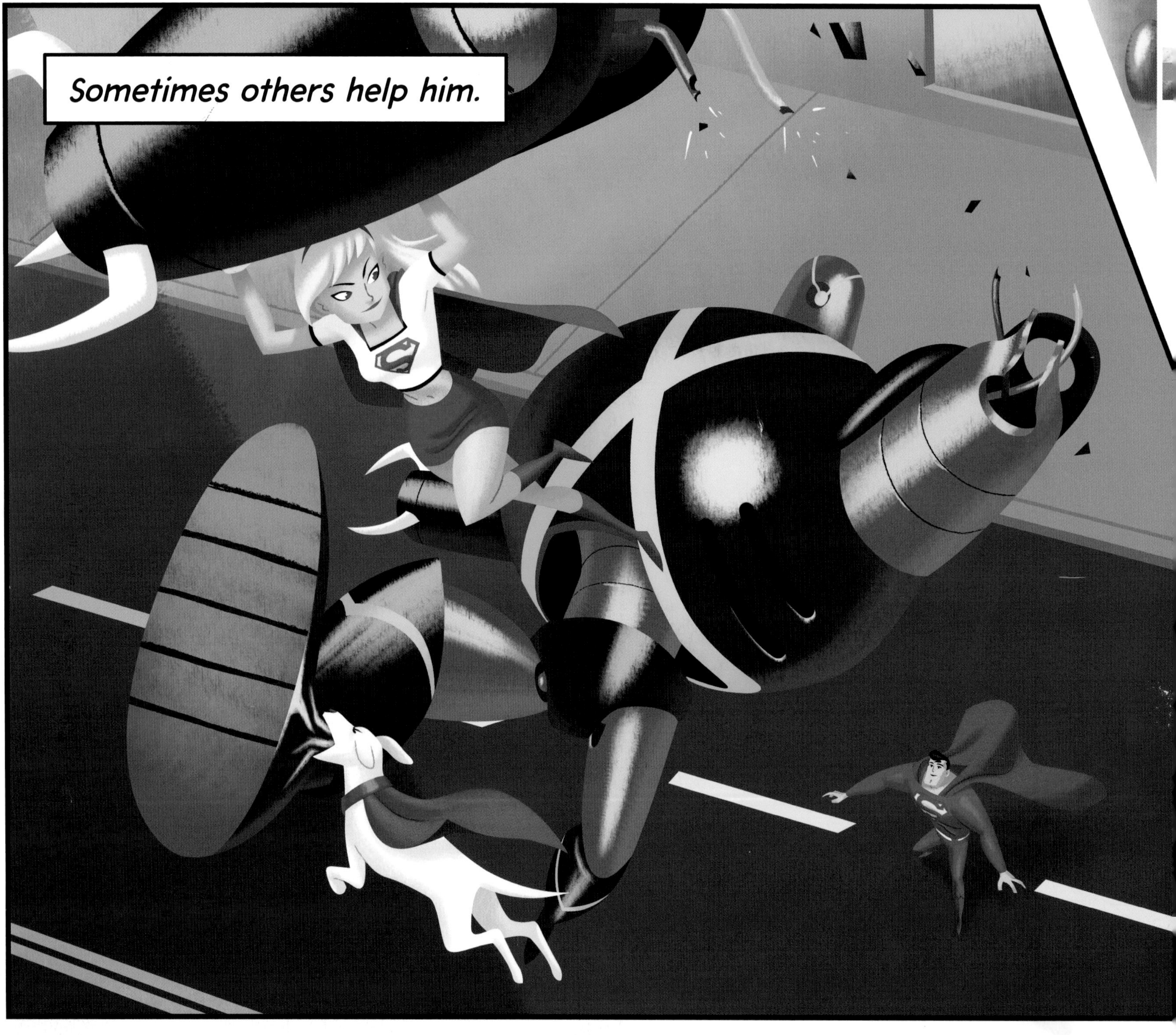
Sometimes others help him.

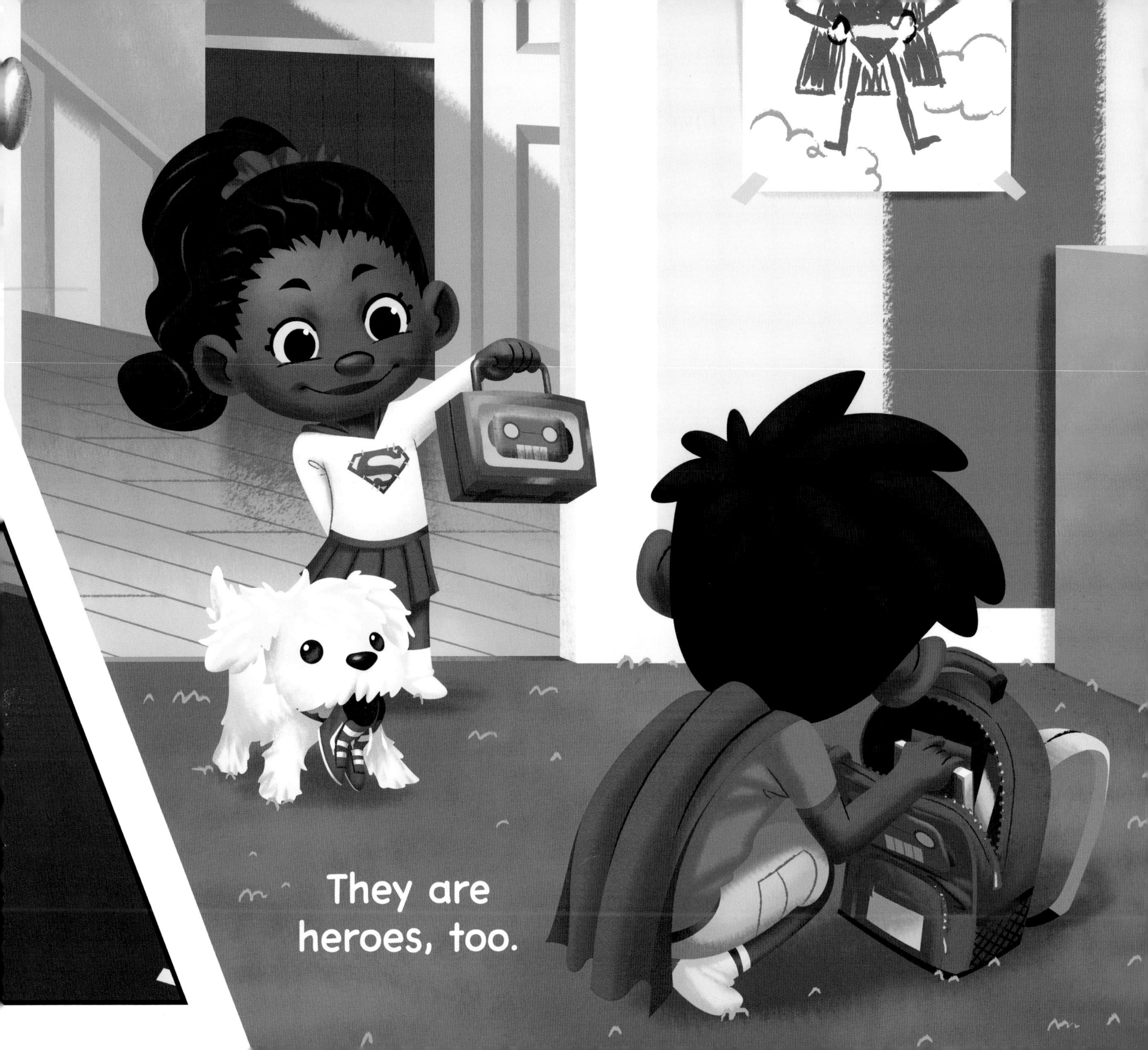

They are
heroes, too.

With super-strength, nothing can stop him!

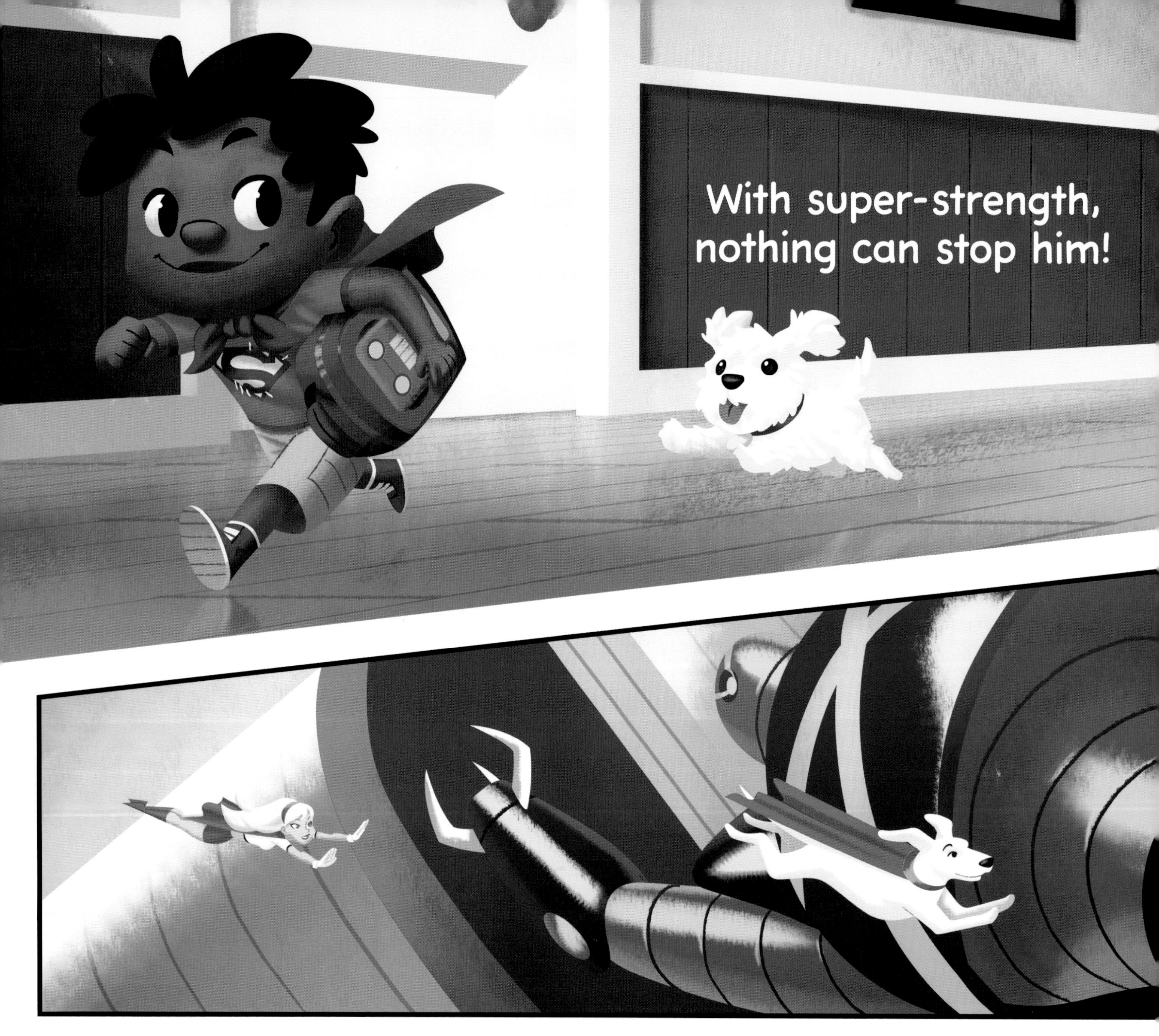

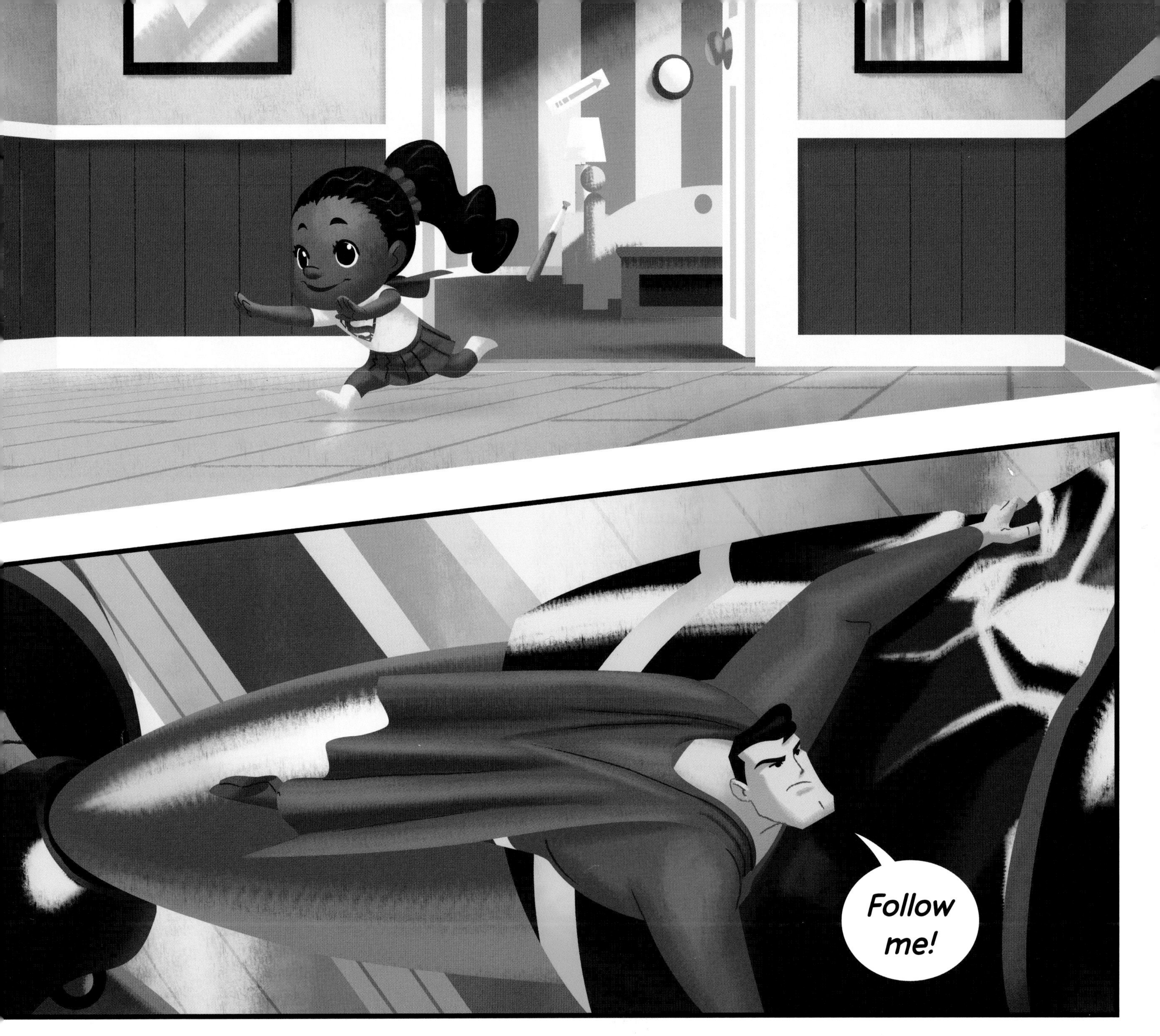
Follow me!

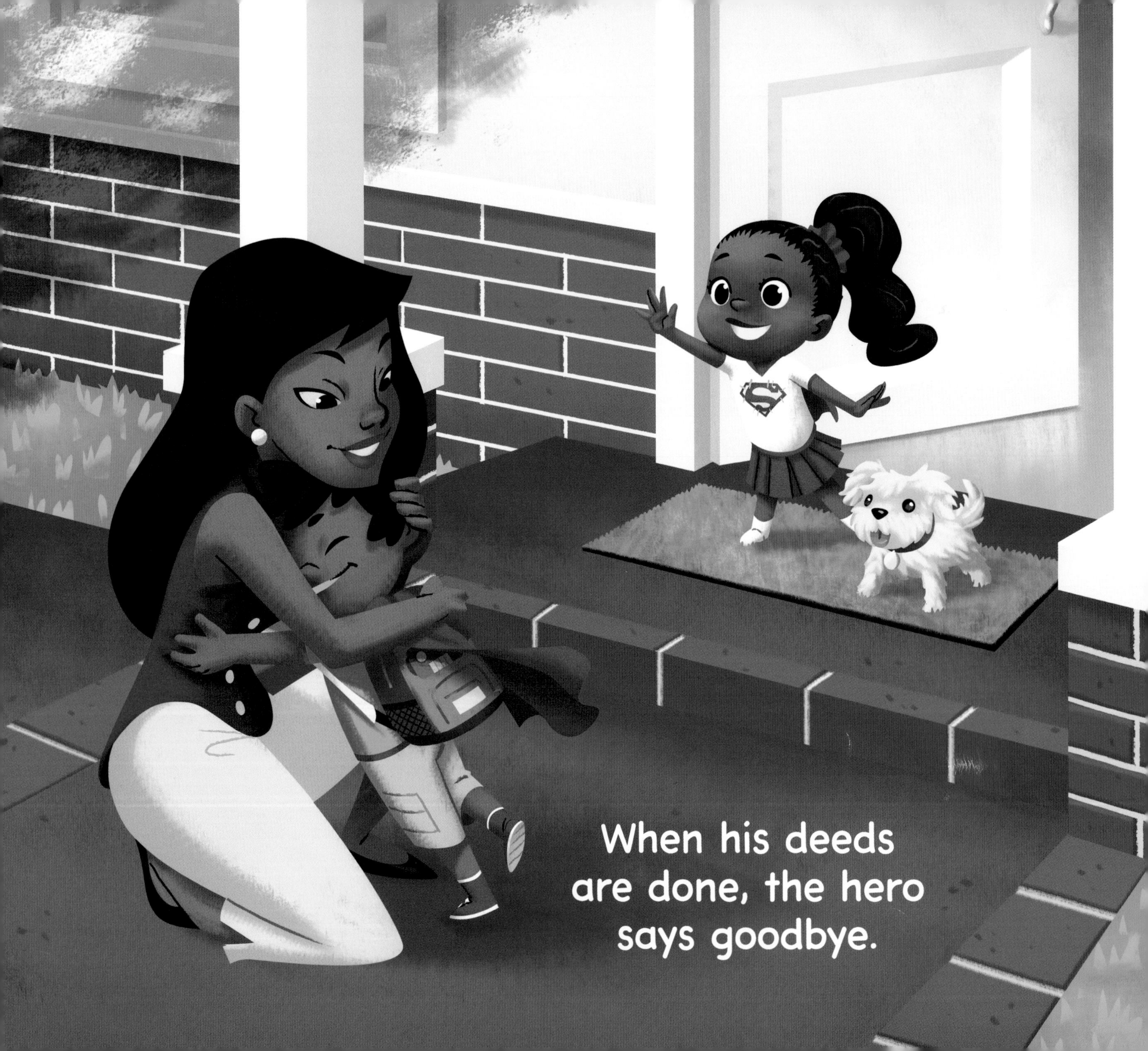

When his deeds
are done, the hero
says goodbye.

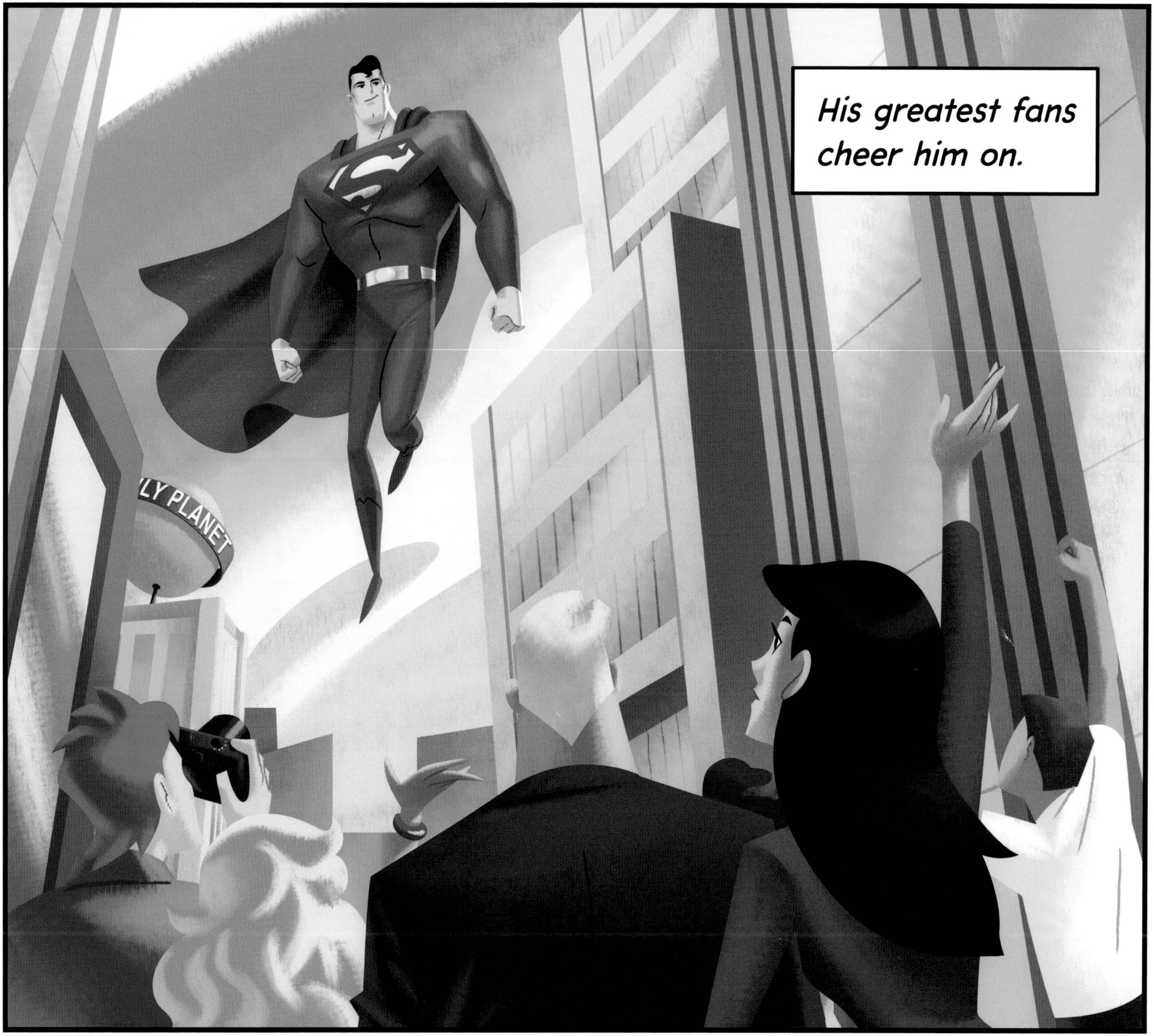
His greatest fans cheer him on.

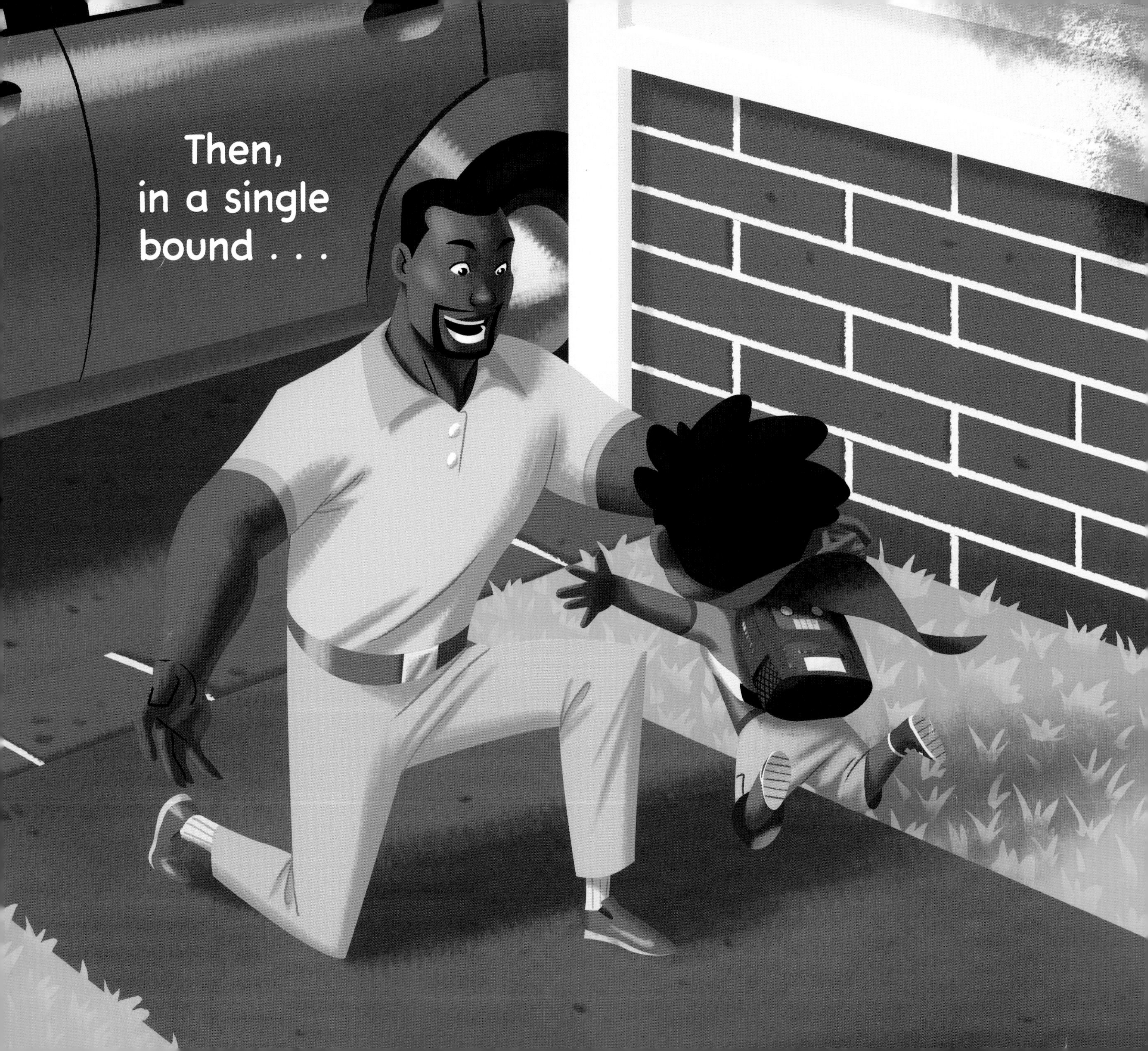

Then,
in a single
bound . . .

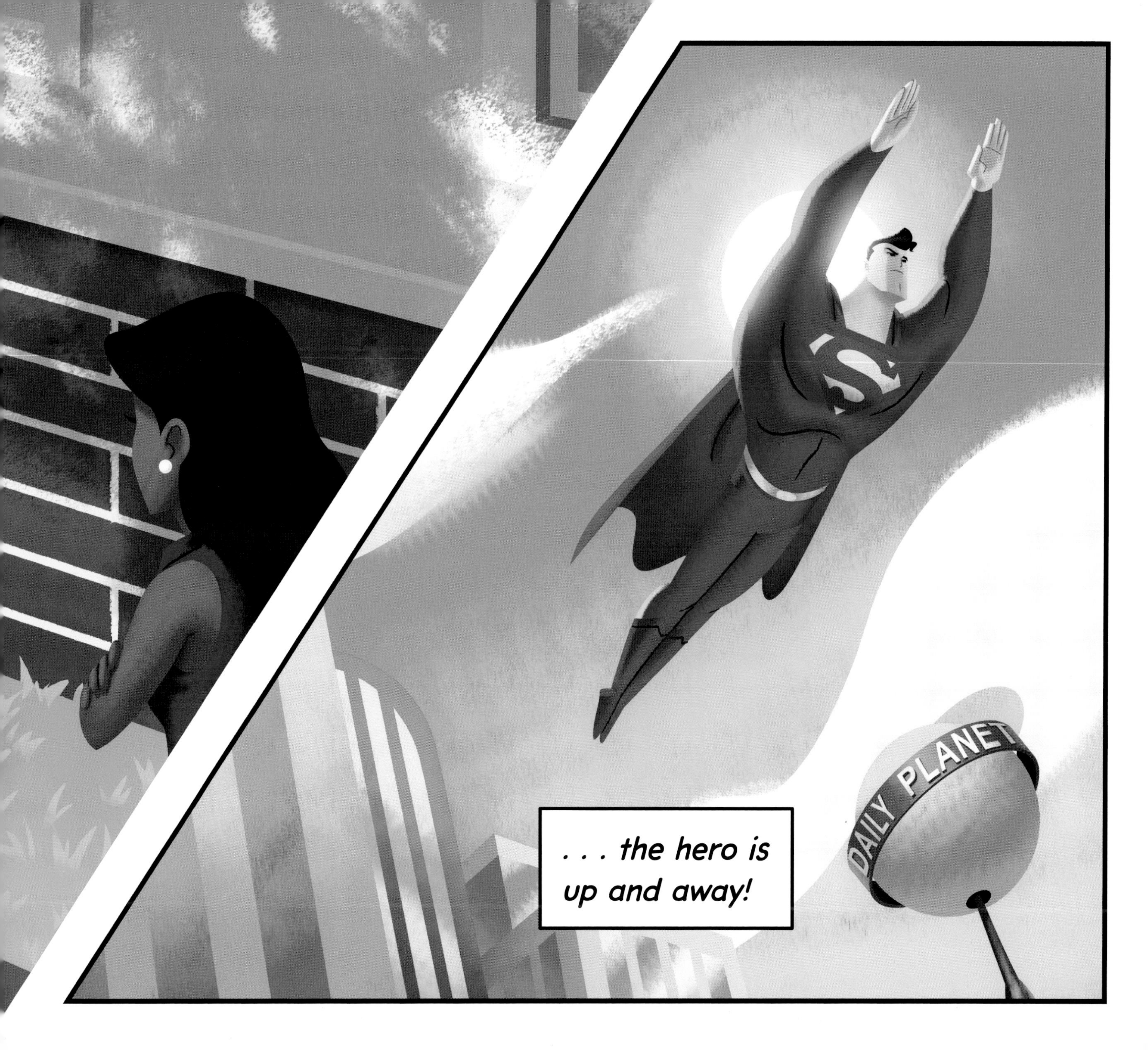
. . . the hero is up and away!
DAILY PLANET

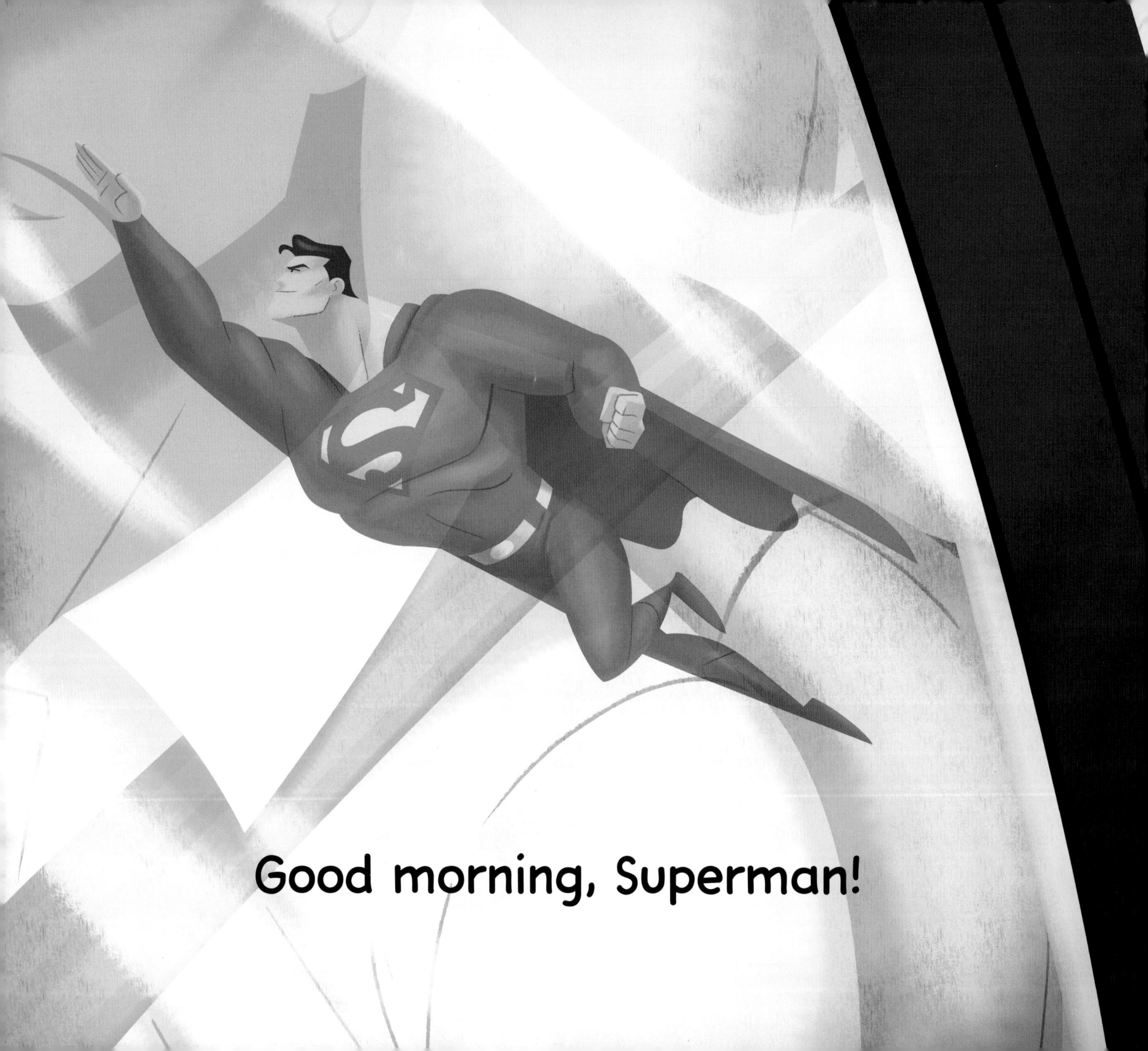

Good morning, Superman!

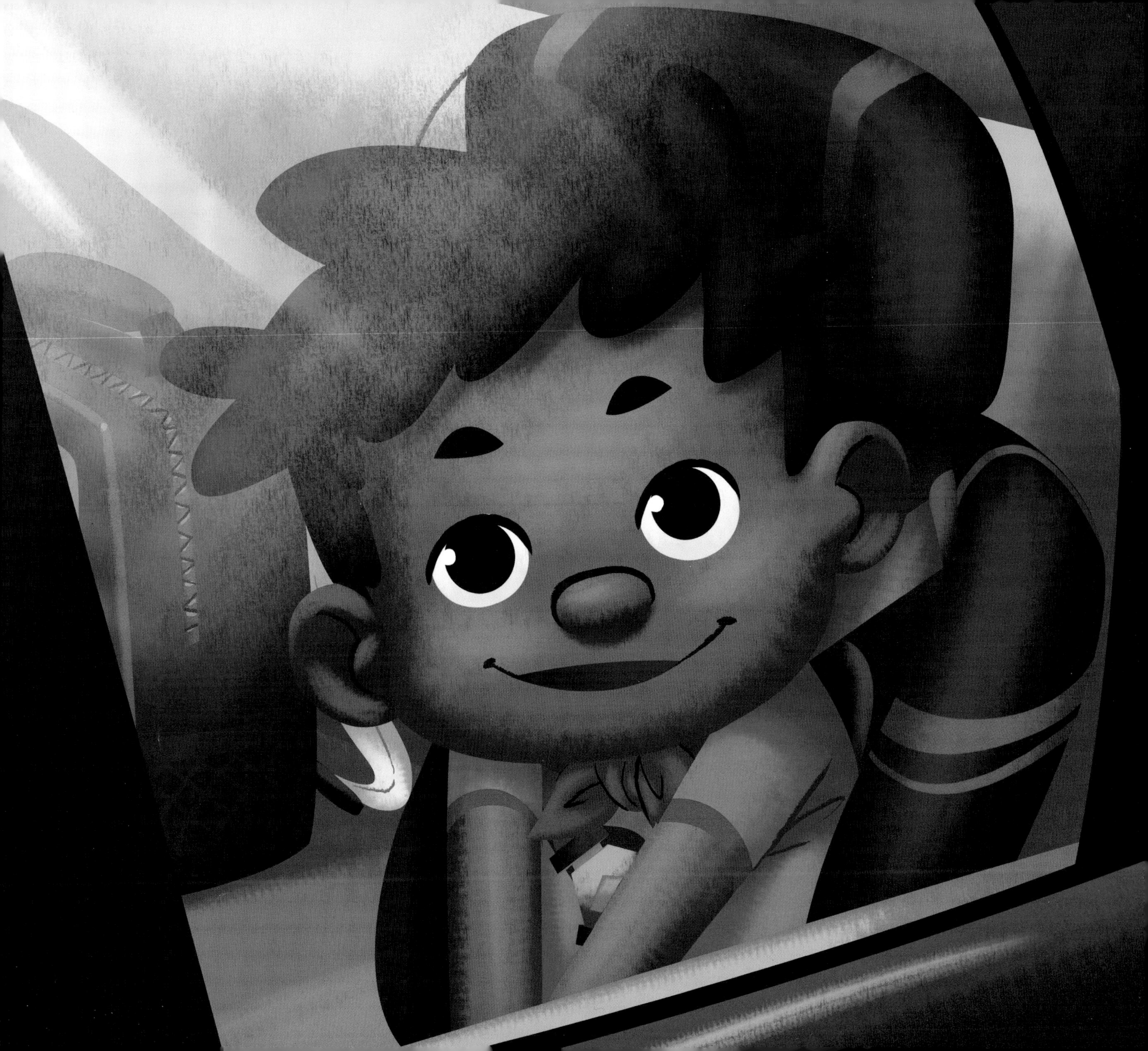

MORNING CHECKLIST!

Go potty

Get dressed

Eat breakfast

Brush teeth

Pack bag

Hugs and kisses

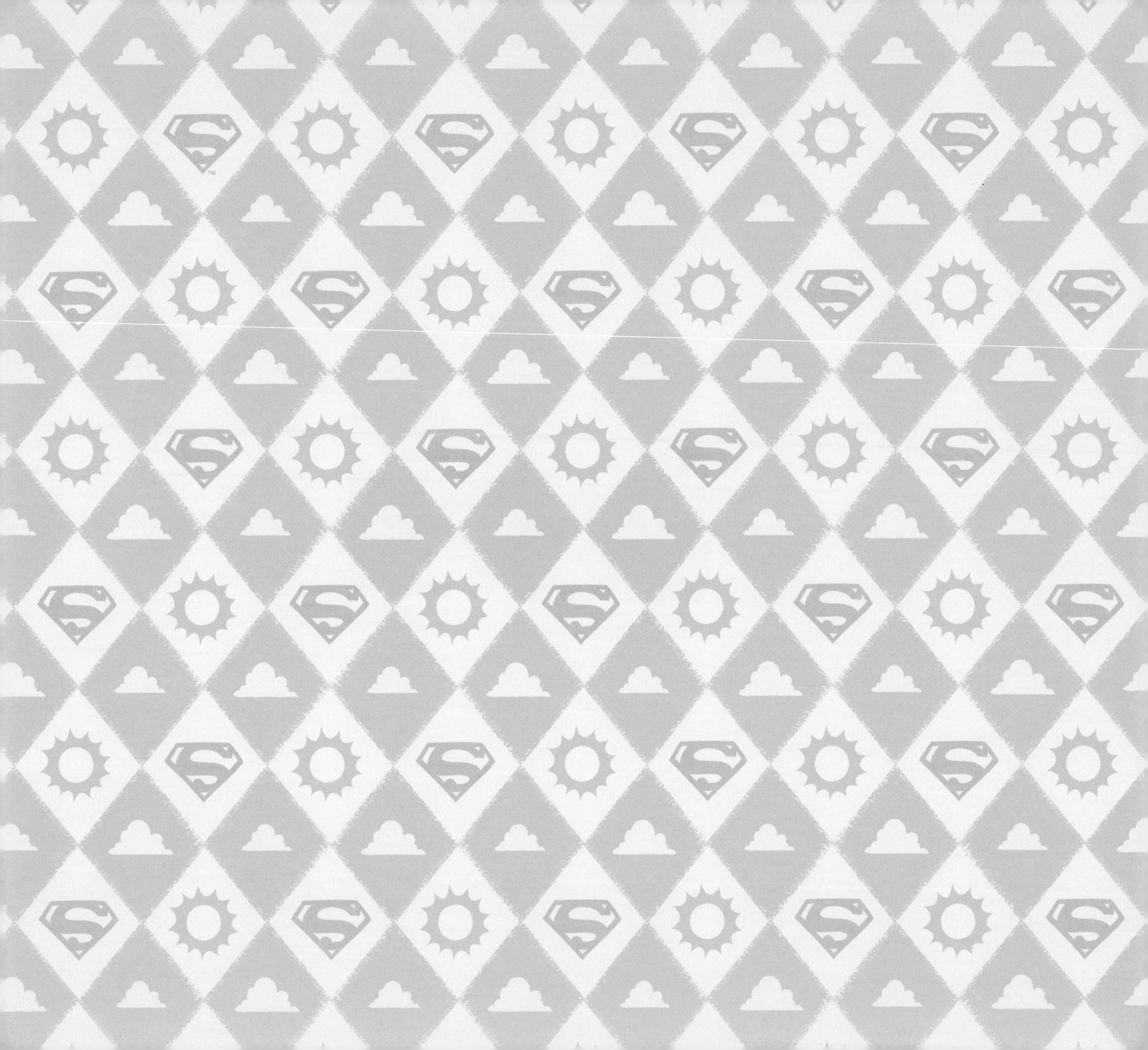